the
Bridesmaid

A NOVELLA

JULIA
LONDON

sourcebooks
casablanca

Published by Sourcebooks Casablanca, an imprint of Sourcebooks, Inc.
P. O. Box 4410, Naperville, Illinois 60567-4410
(630) 961-3900
Fax: (630) 961-2168
www.sourcebooks.com

Library of Congress Cataloging-in-Publication data is on file with the publisher.

Printed and bound in the United States of America.
VP 10 9 8 7 6 5 4 3 2 1

Dedicated to every traveler stranded with me for eight hours when O'Hare International Airport shut down because of storms. Except the guy who took up two seats with his backpack and carry-on, and three plugs for his computer, cell phone, and iPad. Not him. Everyone but him.

Happy travels, Julia

Chapter 1

IT WAS BAD ENOUGH THAT THE DRESS WAS A poufy plantation ball gown number, complete with a sash and apron in a disturbing shade of peach, but it also wouldn't fit in Kate's suitcase. Which meant she was going to have to carry it on the plane. Which she had explained to Lisa when they'd shopped for the bridesmaid gowns six months ago.

"But I *love* it!" Lisa had said, and had made Kate turn around one more time on the little pedestal in the bridal salon.

It was puzzling to Kate. Lisa was her cousin and her best friend. She was pretty and so very stylish. Kate had always wished she were as stylish as Lisa. She'd always admired the way Lisa went after things she wanted, her generosity and kindness, her fabulous sense of humor. But Kate did not care for the way Lisa tended to flip out at the first sign of pressure, or the way she'd latched on to a vision for her wedding that defied logic.

Lisa wanted a plantation wedding. In Seattle. And of course Lisa had bought a slinky mermaid wedding gown for herself. But for her sister Lori, and Kate, her maid of honor, she'd insisted on the peach monstrosities, with clunky platform shoes. Plus, she had the most appalling idea that Kate and Lori would wear their hair in French twists from which peach ribbons would cascade. "Like morning mist," Lisa had said dreamily.

"Like morning puke," Kate's little sister Cassidy had bluntly countered.

Kate had complained to her mother, whose sister had given birth to Lisa and Lori. But Kate's mother was only mildly sympathetic. "It's Lisa's wedding. If she wants that kind of dress, she can have it. When you get married, you can make her wear purple or something."

As there was no prospect of that in sight for Kate, revenge purple didn't seem like a real option.

"And besides, I happen to like peach," her mother had added.

Kate hated the dress, but this morning, she hated it with a passion so strong she might have launched missiles, because she couldn't even get the damn thing into the garment bag—the *pink* garment bag—for the flight from New York to Seattle. It was too poufy.

Kate glanced at the clock; she had an hour before a car arrived to whisk her off to the airport. She still had *so* many things to do. She was not the most organized person on the planet.

She was shoving another pair of shoes into her suitcase when her cell phone rang. "Hi, Mother," she said, hurrying to turn down the TV blaring in the background. "Can't talk long, a car is coming."

"I was calling to see if your flight was on time."

"Yep," Kate said as she frantically sorted through her jewelry box. At least she thought the flight was on time—she hadn't gotten any alerts on her phone. "Why?"

"I'm worried about that storm."

"Storm? What storm?" Kate turned around to her TV. The weatherman was gesturing to a big swath of purple across the middle of the country. It was nowhere near New York. "Are you talking about that?" Kate asked, pointing to a TV her mother couldn't see. "That's Kansas. Or Missouri. One of those corn states."

"It's a huge late-season snowstorm between you and us. Everything is shut down. It's global warming, you know. Greenhouse emissions."

Every inch of rain, every snowflake was now

classified as global warming by Kate's mother. Nevertheless, the storm was not in New York. "It's okay," Kate said impatiently. "They'll just fly over or around it. Not to worry, Mom! I'm on my way!"

"I hope so. It would be devastating if the maid of honor didn't make it. Lisa would explode and die, I think. And it seems like every time you fly home, something happens."

"I have flown home once since I moved to New York, and there was a thirty-minute delay. That's just part of flying these days." Kate had moved to New York six months ago to take a job as an assistant editor at a big publishing house. It was a dream job for an English major. Kate had dreamed of being in publishing since high school, when she'd read *A Clockwork Orange*. Until that book, she hadn't understood how lyrical and powerful story-telling could be, and after that book, she wanted to be a part of it. The pay for assistant editors sucked, but Kate loved it. Loved it, loved it, loved it. And she loved New York. "Listen, I really have to go," she said.

"We'll see you at the airport. Have a safe flight, honey."

Kate clicked off and threw her phone and charger in her purse. And then, through some miracle of physics, managed to shove the bridesmaid dress into the hanging bag, which ballooned to twice its size. Kate cursed Lisa once more, slung her tote bag over her shoulder, wrangled the unwieldy garment bag under her arm, and began to lug her suitcase down to the street from her third-floor walk-up.

Missy Weaten gave Joe a kiss on the cheek. "Call me when you get back to New York, okay?"

"You bet," Joe said, and half fell, half stood from her car at the train station. Bleary-eyed, he watched her as she drove away. He wondered what exactly had happened last night between them. He was fairly certain nothing had, given his high state of inebriation several hours ago, but then again, he was Joe Firretti. He was a red-blooded man, and when opportunity presented itself—even when Missy Weaten presented herself—sometimes, things happened.

He noticed an elderly couple staring at him. He gave them a half smile, ran his fingers through his hair, then straightened his suit coat. He pulled his bag behind him into the train station.

He was not really the type to get wasted the way he had last night. But his pals from work had taken him out for a spectacular send-off. He was on his way to a new job, a fantastic job. A job that came along once in a lifetime. Joe knew it. The financial firm where he worked knew it. The financial firm in Seattle that had extended the very generous offer of employment knew it. Joe would be heading up the technology side of a major international bank.

He had not intended to leave quite this soon for Seattle, but then the bank's head honcho had flown in from Switzerland, and they'd told Joe it was imperative that he meet the CEO while he was available. So Joe had moved his departure up a week. He'd put a deposit down on an apartment and had arranged to have his things picked up and moved to Seattle the next week.

Hoozah.

He stepped up to the ticket machine, rubbed his face with his hands, and glanced at his watch. He had three hours before his plane left, plenty of time to get to Newark and get through security.

He bought his ticket, made his way down to the train, and climbed on board. He wished he'd eaten something. Last night had been a whirl of bars and restaurants and blonde women and no food that he recalled. He hoped he hadn't said anything to Missy to make her think that after two years of her coming on to him, he'd changed his mind. Just to make sure, he'd email her later and thank her for the send-off, then move on.

He was moving on; yes, he was. That's what Joe wanted. He was almost 99 percent sure that's what he wanted. He knew he wanted a bigger opportunity, something great. He knew he wanted to advance in his career. He wanted… *something*. Something. Joe wasn't quite sure what it was, but he felt as close to "it" as he ever had.

At Newark, he made his way into the airport in the middle of a great blob of humanity. Jesus, it was crowded. He maneuvered his way up to the airline kiosk, past grandmas with their belly bags, past crying babies and little kids who ran without looking, past harried business travelers like him.

When he reached the kiosk, he punched the screen as he had a thousand times before, going quickly through the required entries. Something pink was in his peripheral vision, darting in and out, in and out. He glanced at the kiosk directly to his right and saw a woman with shoulder-length blonde hair, an enormous suitcase, and an even larger pink garment bag. At least he thought it was a garment bag. It was hard to make out; it was bloated and huge and reminded him of a life raft.

She was trying to hold on to all of it as she used one finger to jab at the screen.

Joe pulled out his license and held it up to the airline attendant. She handed him his boarding pass. "The flight is delayed about an hour," she said. "Gate 12."

"No, come on," Joe whined. "Not today. I had a late night last night, and the last thing I want is to be hanging out in a crowded airport with all of them," he said, jerking his thumb over his shoulder. He smiled at the attendant.

She did not return his smile. "It's better than listening to people complain about it all day, trust me. A big storm is cutting across the country. A lot of flights have been canceled. Honestly? You'll be lucky to get out."

"Great," Joe muttered. He sighed, took the boarding pass, and moved away from the kiosk. He inadvertently stepped on the giant pink raft when he did.

"Hey!" the woman said.

"Sorry," Joe muttered, and shimmied around her, the pink raft, and the blue bag that looked as if it could hold a small house.

After an interminable wait in the security line, Joe fit his belt back through the loops of his pants, returned his shoes to his feet, and wandered through the terminal, looking for a coffee shop. He ordered a cup of joe, black and thick. He downed it, then collapsed into a chair at the gate. He leaned back, intending to doze, when something knocked against the back of his head. He sat up with a start and turned around, just in time to see that pink raft go sailing by. What had gotten him was the woman's tote bag, draped over her shoulder.

Unbelievable.

Joe stood up and went in search of a calmer place to nap before his plane left.

He found a place, but his nap was a fitful one, due to all the announcements of cancellations and delays. Still, Joe felt a little better when he woke later and stretched out his legs and his arms above his head. He squinted at his gate; they were boarding. Hallelujah—he'd get out of this pit after all. He sauntered to the boarding line, maneuvering once again through even more clumps of people. It almost seemed as if they were being pumped into the airport in groups of twos and threes.

He was among the first to board, thanks to his frequent flyer miles, and settled in to an aisle seat on the same aisle as an elderly woman who had her attention turned to the window. The flight attendant announced to those coming onboard that the flight was completely full and to quickly take their seats. Must be some storm, Joe thought absently, and flipped through the *SkyMall* magazine.

He was sure another person could not squeeze

onto that plane when he saw the pink raft inch its way on board. He watched as the woman and a flight attendant worked to shove the raft into the tiny garment closet. It took both of them and a lot of discussion, but finally, they managed to get the raft in and get the door shut.

The woman was smiling when she stopped at Joe's row. "I think that's my seat," she said, pointing to the middle seat.

What were the odds? "Sure," Joe said, and stood up to allow her to pass.

Her big tote bag knocked into him as she shimmied into the row.

It seemed to take her an inordinate amount of time to get situated, trying her bag beneath the seat in front of her in various configurations, then finally using both boots to push it under.

And then she started to chat.

"Whew," she said. "This is one crowded flight."

He did not respond. It was his experience that the less he said, the less people tried to talk to him, as he really had no desire to make friends on every flight he took. He preferred to be left alone, to work or sleep or listen to music if he wanted.

But the chick sitting next to him, cute though she was with her bright green eyes and silky blonde hair, *talked*. She said, apparently to no one, that she didn't like to fly, but that she had to get to a wedding. When that elicited no response, she asked Joe why he was on his way to Seattle.

"Job."

"Job!" she said, and nodded as if she approved. "What sort of job?"

"Computers." God, was there any way to cut this off without being a complete jerk? Joe realized he suddenly had a raging headache.

"You will love Seattle. I'm from there. It doesn't rain as much as you think—it can be really nice."

He hadn't said one word about rain. "Okay."

"It's really beautiful."

"Yeah… I've been a few times."

"Oh. Okay." She settled back, helping herself to the armrest between them.

"Gooooood afternoon, ladies and gentlemen," said a voice over the intercom. "We've got some light turbulence ahead associated with this big blizzard that's cutting across the country. We're going to ask the flight attendants to remain in their seats until we feel it's safe for them to be up and around. In the meantime, please stay in your seats with your seat belts fastened until we turn off the seat-belt sign."

"But I'm starving. I wanted peanuts," the woman next to him muttered.

The pilot said some other things that were lost

on Joe because he had closed his eyes and was drifting off again. He apparently drifted hard, because he was only vaguely aware of takeoff. He didn't know how long he dozed, but he was rudely awakened by a rather severe drop in altitude that caused everyone in the cabin to cry out.

"Folks, we're heading into some turbulence. Please stay in your seats with your seat belts securely fastened," the pilot said again, which was reiterated by the more urgent voice of the flight attendant.

Joe sat up and glanced to his left. The woman in the center seat had a mound of little peanut bags on her tray. She noticed him looking at them and picked one up. "You want one? They came by while you were snoring."

"I was snoring?" he asked, mortified.

"A little." She shook the peanut bag at him again. "You want?"

"No. Thanks."

She shrugged and, with one hand, swiped the peanuts into her bag and lifted her tray table.

At the same moment, they hit another pocket of turbulence that made the plane shake. The woman grabbed the armrest, her eyes wide. "What the hell?"

"It's just turbulence," Joe said with the authority of a seasoned traveler, but he was wondering the same thing. That was a pretty big drop.

"Hey folks, I've got some news," the pilot's disembodied voice said above them. "What we've got here is the convergence of a Canadian cold front and a tropical storm coming up from the Atlantic that's just creating havoc across the country. Unfortunately, this big late-season blizzard had some pretty impressive ice associated with it, and we have an instrument that's acting a little wacky. We're going to land in Dallas and have a look."

"Oh no," the woman muttered, her head bouncing back against the seat back. "No, no, no, *no*. I *have* to be in Seattle."

No, Joe silently agreed.

"Don't worry, we're going to get you to Seattle," the pilot said, apparently able to hear the hue and cry that was welling up in the cabin. "But we want to get you there safely."

"I don't care how you get me there," she muttered. "Just *get* me there."

Chapter 2

FROM THE SMALL SLIVER OF WINDOW THAT KATE could see, it looked as if every plane flying across the United States had diverted to Dallas. Beneath slate gray skies, planes of all sizes were lined up on the tarmac, waiting for available gates.

They'd been waiting for two hours. Two excruciatingly long hours in which she'd been squeezed in between a grandma with generous hips and a man with impossibly broad shoulders. With the latter, Kate was engaged in a silent battle for the armrest. Every time she moved, he popped his elbow onto it. Every time he turned around to look for the flight attendant—which was often—she reclaimed it. What was it about men that made them think they had some inalienable right to the armrests?

He sighed again, loudly and with great exasperation, and then kicked his feet around under the seat in front of him like a little boy who had grown frustrated that he could not find a comfortable position.

Kate rolled her eyes, opened her purse, and took out a bag of peanuts.

His attention snapped instantly to her.

She opened the bag, fished out one peanut, and popped it into her mouth.

He was riveted.

Kate ate another peanut and glanced at him from the corner of her eye.

His gaze narrowed; his vivid blue eyes zeroed in on hers, silently challenging. Kate munched her peanuts and considered him. He was cute, she thought. Dark, wavy hair, long enough to tuck behind his ears. Sexy lips. Yep, he was so cute that Kate momentarily forgot he was an armrest hog.

His gaze fell to her bag of peanuts, and then to her purse.

"Would you like some?" Kate asked pleasantly.

He clenched his jaw. He was trying very hard not to want them, she could see that, and she couldn't help but smile brightly. "I have several bags."

"Maybe that's why they ran out of bags for everyone else a half hour ago."

"Testy," she said with a shrug and ate another peanut. "My philosophy is, you snooze, you lose. In your case, literally." She laughed at her own joke, then reached into her purse and rummaged around, finding another bag. She held it up. "Do you want one... Wait, what did you say your name was?"

"I didn't," he said tightly.

She wiggled the bag of peanuts.

"*Joe*," he said.

"I'm Kate." She smiled and handed him the bag. "Knock yourself out."

"Thanks," he said, and when he lifted his arm to take the bag from her, Kate firmly planted her elbow on the armrest.

He tore the bag open, tipped it upside down, and dumped all the peanuts in his mouth. One would think they'd been on the plane without food for days instead of hours.

He'd just wadded the empty wrapper into a tight little ball when the engines suddenly fired. Cries of relief went up from the cabin as the plane shuddered forward. The captain, Kate noticed, didn't say anything. He was sick of it, too.

The plane slid up to a gate, and although the flight attendant instructed the passengers to remain seated with their seat belts fastened until the captain had turned off the illuminated sign, no one listened. There was a mad push to get off that plane, a lot of shouting for people to hurry up. Joe popped up from his seat instantly. He was cute *and* tall, an inch or two over six feet, Kate thought. He was also trim and muscular, and looked as if he did a lot of working out.

He blocked the aisle, gesturing impatiently for Kate and the grandma to get out, too.

"Oh! *Thank* you," Kate said gratefully, and hurried forward to rescue her bridesmaid dress, which took some wresting out of the tiny space, much to the annoyance of everyone behind her. Once Kate had freed it, she hoisted the thing on her back and slugged her tote bag over her shoulder. She marched forward, anxious to be as far from that plane as she could get.

Unfortunately, the plane disgorged its passengers into an overcrowded terminal dripping with bad mojo and body odor. In the melee of angry passengers and harried airline personnel shouting at everyone to calm down, Kate lost sight of Joe. She thought she spotted him on the other side of the airline desk helping the grandma into a seat, but the swelling crowd quickly obstructed Kate's view.

And really, she had other pressing issues on her mind at that moment: a bathroom. She fought her way across the wide corridor from the gate to stand in line at the women's bathroom with what felt like another person on her back and a bowling ball in her shoulder bag.

Several minutes later, when she emerged once again into the terminal, it seemed, impossibly, as if things were even more chaotic. She was dismayed to see the number of cancellations on the arrivals and departures board. Lisa was going to have a complete meltdown if Kate was delayed. Her cousin was not exactly the most laid-back woman in the world.

The attendant at the airline desk was making an announcement, but Kate couldn't make out a word she was saying. So she pushed her way through the crowd and found herself next to a very thin, very put-together blonde. The blonde's fingers were flying across her phone.

"Excuse me," Kate said. "Sorry to bother you, but did you happen to hear what they said?"

"Yes," the woman said without looking up. "We are to collect our baggage and they will try and reroute us." She suddenly looked up. "But don't get your hopes up. The news is reporting that the air traffic controllers are going on strike at midnight."

"Wait, *what*?" Kate exclaimed, completely startled by that news and the fact that a mass of humanity had turned around and was starting to move in one fleshy wall toward the baggage claim.

"You haven't heard?" Blondie asked. "Big freak blizzard across one half the country, and air traffic controllers are about to strike. We're screwed."

"Oh no," Kate said. "I cannot be screwed. I *can't*. I have to be at a wedding!"

"If I were you, I'd see about getting a hotel around here somewhere. I don't think anyone is going anywhere. Good luck," she added, and put herself in the people stream to baggage claim.

This could not be happening. Lisa would flip out, and Kate really didn't want to live the rest of her life and possibly die at DFW airport. She frantically dug in her bag for her phone as she moved with the wall of people toward baggage claim.

At the baggage carousel, Kate was able to prop up her pink garment bag to stand directly beside her so that she could call Lisa. *"Hey!"* she said brightly when Lisa answered. "How's the bride?"

"Where *are* you?" Lisa demanded. "I've been trying to get hold of you all day!"

"You have?" Kate asked. "I'm on my way—"

"Oh God, that's right," Lisa sighed. "I forgot you were flying in today. I just really need to talk to you," she said. "I don't… something is going on."

Lisa clearly had not heard about the storm or the impending strike, Kate thought, which was good. But she didn't need any additional drama right now. "What's up?" she asked reluctantly.

"I don't know if I want to do this," Lisa said. "Is that awful?"

"Do what?" Kate asked, and was knocked from the back as an impatient man went barreling past her. She managed to catch herself and her dress.

"Get married," Lisa said impatiently. "I mean, I love him, at least I think I do, but honestly, sometimes I wonder if I really, truly know what love is, Kate! What if there is someone else out there who is a better match? How do I know for certain that Kiefer is the one?"

Lord. Kate was not alarmed; she was annoyed. Lisa had always been like this, always creating drama, always second-guessing everything about her life. Kate's aunt—Lisa's mom—said she was a dreamer. Kate's mom said Lisa was a little wishy-washy. Kate thought Lisa was just straight-up nuts most of the time, with a little deranged thrown in to make things interesting. "Are you kidding, Lisa? Your wedding is in two days. Two days!"

"I know, I know," Lisa moaned. "But we had this discussion last night—well, more of a fight, really. Anyway, he said there were certain things I ought to understand by now, and I said, sometimes I think I understand too much, and he said, what's *that* supposed to mean—"

The baggage carousel suddenly cranked to life, drowning out Lisa's recounting of the fight.

"Okay, listen," Kate said. "You have to take a

breath. I'll be there soon, okay? You're just having bridal jitters, that's all. Everyone gets them. But Lisa, do *not* flip out. Do you understand? Don't flip out! Don't do anything stupid until I get there."

"Okay," Lisa said, but she didn't sound particularly on board with that plan.

"Is that a promise?"

"Sort of."

"Okay, well look, I'll call you in a few hours. Right now, I have to go. I have to… change planes," Kate said quickly.

"Call me as soon as you can," Lisa demanded.

She would call her all right, Kate thought. If she lugged this damn Scarlett O'Hara dress across a freak snowstorm and an air traffic controller strike for nothing, she could not be held responsible for what she would do to her most beloved cousin and best friend.

She spotted her suitcase coming around. Naturally, it was on top of other bags. She pushed her way into the rail, then muscled her heavy bag off the merry-go-round. She knew she shouldn't have brought so many shoes.

With her belongings all around her now, and the dress propped up beside her, Kate pondered what she should do next.

"What is that, anyway, your own personal flotation device?" a male voice asked.

Kate had to lean forward and around her garment bag to see her ex-seatmate. Joe looked completely unruffled by all the airport drama. At his foot was a gray suitcase, only half the size of hers. "One can never be too prepared, I always say," Kate said. "Where's yours?"

He actually smiled at that. "If I am going to be some place that requires a personal flotation device, I don't think my flotation device is going to make much of a difference."

Kate smiled. "You make a good argument. So did you hear? Air traffic controller strike is coming."

"I heard," he said. "So maybe you do have the right idea," he said, looking at her garment bag. "Because if that happens, the only way out of Dallas might be via raft."

"Hey!" a woman said behind her.

Kate turned around to see Blondie standing next to her, still furiously typing away on her phone, two bags stacked neatly beside her. "So some people are trying to get to Austin or Houston from here to see if they can get out. They're further south and can route around the storm through Phoenix or someplace like that."

"Oh," Kate said. She was aware that Joe had

suddenly moved closer, was standing at her back, listening. "How are they getting there?"

"Rental cars," Blondie said, and looked up. "Just down that hall."

"Thank you," Kate said. "Did you get one?"

"Not me. I am checking into the Gaylord and getting a massage. You should really do the same."

"I'll think about it," Kate said. She did not relish the thought of driving to Austin or Houston, not without at least seeing what the airline came up with. But neither did she like the idea of leaving the airport to check into a hotel. She turned around to speak to Joe, but he was gone—she spotted him striding in the direction of the rental car agencies. Apparently he thought that was the only way out of here, and the fact that he did made an impression on Kate. Maybe he knew something she didn't know.

She gathered up her mélange of luggage and hurried after him.

Joe was in the Dollar Rent A Car line, so Kate went to the Budget line, determined to get a car before he did. But as she waited, she noticed that voices were getting louder and louder at her counter. People in front of her were sighing loudly and with frustration, muttering under their breath.

She checked Joe's position at Dollar and was startled to see him looking at her. She quickly looked away. The couple in front of her suddenly whirled about with stormy expressions. "Is something wrong?" Kate asked.

"They don't have any cars!" the woman said angrily. "I can*not* believe they don't have any cars! They are a *car rental company*," she said emphatically.

"No one has any cars," said a man behind Kate. "They've all been grabbed."

"Then why don't they bring them from other places?" the woman demanded, as if it were perfectly reasonable to expect that the car rental agency could have anticipated this disaster.

Kate began to gather her things. It was back to the airline, she guessed. "I heard that Hertz had a few cars," the man behind her said.

That brought Kate's head up. She whipped around to look at the Hertz counter, and when she did, she noticed Joe was looking at her again. His gaze followed hers to the Hertz counter. And then he looked at her again.

Kate suddenly lurched in the direction of Hertz, dragging her garment bag and kicking her tote bag in front of her until she could dip down and pick it up as she sprinted across the tile floor. By the time she had picked it up, however, Joe had made an acrobatic leap over the blue rope of Dollar Rent A

Car and was sprinting ahead of her in the direction of Hertz.

Kate angrily used her garment bag as a blocker and actually rushed through a couple deep in conversation to shorten the distance she had to cover to beat Joe. But she was weighed down with her things, and he obviously possessed some freakish natural athletic talent, because he didn't even look winded as he sailed to a spot in line in front of her. He turned around and smiled at her. "Sorry, but I have to get to Seattle."

"So do I!" she said sternly. "I have to get to a wedding!"

"And I have to get to the opportunity of a lifetime. It's every man for himself."

"That is *not* fair!" Kate cried.

"Who said natural disasters were fair?" He smiled at her.

"Do *not* smile at me," she said angrily. "Do. Not. *Smile*."

But he did smile. He smiled with twinkly blue eyes as if she amused him, as if they were standing at some bar in the middle of happy hour instead of a crowded airport in the middle of a natural disaster.

And then the Armrest Hog got the last rental car at DFW.

Chapter 3

THE CAR JOE GOT WAS ROUGHLY THE SIZE OF A pickle jar. He couldn't make the driver's seat go back far enough to accommodate his legs and cursed the idiot who had designed such a stupidly small vehicle.

The guy at the counter had told him Austin had one airport, but Houston had two. Joe had instantly concluded that his odds of getting a flight out had to double with two airports. "How long will it take me to get to Houston?" he asked.

"Three and a half hours on a good day," the man had said.

"Okay. How long on a stupendously bad day?"

The man had laughed. "Have a good trip, sir!" he'd said cheerfully as he handed Joe the keys.

"Too late for that," Joe had muttered, and had stomped out of the office with the keys in hand.

After he'd wedged himself in the car and started

driving—directly into the sun, that was—he was reminded that he had a splitting headache, and after a day of trying to sober up, he was ravenously hungry. In fact, he was surfing his phone for any nearby McDonald's as traffic crawled along, which resulted in him taking a wrong turn.

When Joe looked up, he realized he had just entered the river of vehicles moving at a snail's pace into the terminal. "Ah hell," he muttered, then pounded the steering wheel a few times to let off some frustration.

Traffic into the terminal was barely moving as people drove in to pick up stranded passengers. Joe's fingers drummed impatiently on the steering wheel. He tried to find a radio station, but everyone was talking about the blizzard and the impending strike. He switched that off, then turned his head slightly to shove fingers through his hair. That's when he caught sight of pink in his peripheral vision. He sat up; he could see her on the sidewalk, taking up an entire bench with her pink raft and luggage. Kate herself was sitting with her knees together, her elbows braced against them, her head in her hands, her blonde hair spilling around her shoulders.

"Good luck," he sighed as he inched by. But as he neared the split in the road—right would take him to freedom, away from the terminal, while left would circle back around—he inexplicably went left.

"What are you *doing*?" he shouted at himself. Yes, okay, he'd taken pity on her. For one thing, she was pretty with those eyes and that hair. He had a thing for silky hair. And in spite of the fact that she had no spatial awareness when it came to shared armrests, she seemed nice. After all, she'd given him a bag of peanuts. Last, he had to acknowledge that she was severely handicapped with that pink thing. The least he could do was give her a ride to Houston.

"Consider it your good deed of the day," he muttered to himself as he maneuvered into the lane to pick up passengers. "If you do this good deed, you won't feel too bad when you grab the last seat on some flight to Seattle."

It took another ten minutes to reach the curb. She was now sitting up, her shapely legs, encased in boots and tights, sprawled before her, her head back on the bench and her eyes closed. Joe rolled down the window. "Hey, Kate!" he called out the window.

She sat up with a start and looked wildly about.

Joe honked his horn. "Kate! Over here!"

She realized where he was and stood up, squinting at him warily. "*Joe?*"

"I'm going to Houston. Want to come?"

Now she looked completely suspicious, as if she thought it was some sort of joke, as if someone was going to leap out from behind a bush and announce that she'd been punked. So much for good intentions, Joe thought.

"I just thought I'd offer. But you don't have to go—"

"No!" Kate did a funny little hop. "I mean *yes*! *Yesssss!*"

Now Joe was the one who was startled. She was suddenly dragging her things toward the car. He hopped out and hurried around to help her. "Here," she said, shoving her suitcase at him.

That thing was heavy—what was she carrying, a bunch of bricks? "What is in here?" he asked, lugging it along to the car.

"Shoes," she said breathlessly. "And books."

Joe threw it into the trunk and closed it. Kate was trying to get the pink thing in the backseat. He walked around, intending to help her. "Let me help you."

"Got it!" she said quickly. "It can't get wrinkled." She bent into his car, squirming around as she tried to fit the thing in perfectly.

But the only thing Joe could see was her derriere. He didn't mean to look, but come on, how could her help it? He was a guy, and *that* was a nice derriere. When she'd finally situated the pink raft as she wanted, she backed out, turned around, and looked up at him, pushing her hair back from her face. There was a slender moment when her gaze flicked over his face, and then her eyes narrowed slightly.

She knew he'd been looking.

"What's in there, anyway?" he asked.

"In there? In there is the ugliest, most hideous, god-awful poufy piece of peach taffeta in the history of mankind. But I have to wear it or my cousin will *die*. And I'm not kidding."

Joe smiled. "Okay, then. Let's get out of here, huh?"

"Please," she said primly, and slid very gracefully into the passenger seat of that stupidly small car, and stuffed her shoulder bag in at her feet.

Joe walked around and wedged himself in again, then eased in front of another car.

"I thought we could grab something to eat on the way out," he said. "I don't know about you, but I'm starving."

"Oh, me too!" she said, sinking back into the passenger seat. "I tried to get some yogurt at the food court, but there is nothing left. Nothing! It's like zombies went through and ate everything."

"Zombies don't eat," he said absently as he pulled into traffic.

She looked at him as if she thought he was crazy. "What do you mean, they don't eat?"

"Zombies are dead," he said. "They don't eat. Haven't you ever seen a zombie movie?"

"No."

"No?" Joe had never known a single person who hadn't seen a zombie movie, with the exception of his mother. It was practically a requirement for his generation, which he assumed Kate was part of. "You have to see a zombie movie. Just one. You can't go an entire lifetime without it," he said as they began to inch out of the terminal.

She laughed. "I've made it twenty-eight years without seeing one."

Yeah, well, he would keep his opinions about that to himself. "So how are you at navigating?" he asked, and thrust the one-page map the rental counter had given him in her direction.

She snatched it out of his hand and peered closely. "I happen to be pretty fantastic at navigating. Where are we?"

He pointed to the terminal and the highway they'd be entering. Which they did, about fifteen minutes later, and began to zip along at a top speed of sixty-five miles an hour.

They hadn't gone far when Joe spied the Golden Arches. He veered off the highway and turned into McDonald's.

Kate looked up. Her mouth dropped open. "Wait—you're not going *here*, are you?"

"Yep," he said, and pulled into a parking spot. "I'm hungry, remember?"

"But not McDonald's!"

"What's wrong with Mickey D's?" Joe asked as he unbuckled his seat belt. He knew full well what was wrong with it—he'd had enough girlfriends to know that the nutritional values of the food were not in the acceptable range for sleek New York women.

"You're kidding, right?"

"No."

She gasped. "Calories! Fat!"

He was too hungry to debate it. "You don't look like you have to worry about that," he said gruffly. "And besides, we don't have time for a fine dining experience, remember? So—are you hungry?"

Kate shifted forward and squinted out the front windshield at the restaurant. "Starving," she muttered, and unbuckled her seat belt.

A few minutes later, they were in the car again. Kate, Joe noticed, was wolfing down the burger she'd disdained. She happened to come up for breath and noticed his look of amusement. "Don't judge me," she warned him, and punctuated that with a big bite of burger.

Joe laughed. He liked a woman who could eat. "Bon appétit," he said as he started the car up and backed out of the parking space.

Kate had polished off the burger and the fries she'd bought by the time they neared downtown Dallas and a dizzying display of highways in the sky, looping up and over each other. Just as they began to enter that mess, her phone rang.

"Don't answer it," Joe said. "I'm not sure what road I'm supposed to take."

"45," she said, and bent over, digging through her bag.

"Come on, call them back," he pleaded, but Kate already had the phone in hand.

"Lisa!" she said cheerfully. "What's up?"

"I don't see it. I don't see 45," he said.

Kate pointed out the front window. *"Left,"* she whispered, and Joe wondered if she truly thought that was even remotely helpful.

"Oh, did you hear? Yes, well, not to worry. I'm on my way to Houston right now. Supposedly, planes are still flying out of Houston. Huh? Oh, it's close. Like an hour or something."

"It's at least three hours," Joe said.

Kate waved her hand at him in a manner that Joe believed meant he was not to talk.

"45," he said to her. "Where is it?"

"That's another passenger," Kate said into the phone. "Lisa, can you hold on one minute?" She covered the phone with her hand. "45 is a left exit. *Left!* And it says Houston in big white letters."

"You don't have to be sarcastic," he grumbled, and began the arduous task of slipping a tiny little car across five lanes of much faster and much thicker traffic. The sign, he noticed, did not say Houston.

"So I'll be there in plenty of time—" She paused. She bent her head, rubbed her forehead. "Okay, what did he say?" she asked, and listened attentively. After a few moments, she nodded and said, "Okay, listen, Lisa. Listen to me. Getting married is a big deal. He is probably just a little nervous, right? I mean, he wouldn't have asked you to marry him if he didn't love you and didn't want to spend the rest of his life with you."

"Not necessarily," Joe said.

Kate gasped and jerked her wide-eyed gaze to him.

He shrugged. "I'm just saying," he said casually. "Sometimes, women will put unbelievable pressure on a guy to put a ring on it."

Kate's brows suddenly dipped. She pressed a finger to her lips, and said, "He's kidding. And who is he, anyway? But I know Kiefer, and I know he is crazy about you." She glared at Joe once more. "What?" she suddenly cried. "God, Lisa, can you please not do anything crazy until I get there? Please? You always do this when you get stressed. You freak out about things that aren't even real and make a mess! I will be there in less than twelve hours!" she said.

Joe looked at her and winced a little. He thought she might be overselling things a little.

But Kate glared again and pointed at him and mouthed the words, *Not a word*.

"Okay, thank you," Kate said into the phone. "Go get a massage or something. Just chill out. Relax. Where is Mom, anyway?"

Kate stayed on the phone another couple of minutes, and finally hung up. When she did, she tossed her phone into her bag, folded her arms, and stared at him.

Joe felt a prickly bit of heat under his collar. "What?"

"You know what."

"I was just saying—"

"You don't say that to a bride forty-eight hours before her wedding!" Kate exclaimed, her hands moving wildly. "You don't know her—she's nuts. She can make mountains out of tiny little anthills without as much as a match."

That made absolutely no sense, but Joe wasn't going to point that out. "So what did the groom say?" he asked.

Kate moaned and sank back in her seat. "That he was feeling antsy," she said. "Whatever that means."

Joe knew exactly what it meant. "It means he is feeling antsy. That's it. I mean, think about it—he has to put on a monkey suit and stand up before a bunch of people and say things he wouldn't say to his best friend, you know? That would make any guy antsy." He should know. He once came dangerously close to it himself. Sort of close. He hadn't actually asked Mona to marry him, but he'd *thought* about it, and just thinking about it had made him antsy.

"That's ridiculous. If you love someone, you ought to be able to say it. Like a grown-up."

"I am sure he can *say* it," Joe said. "Like a grown-up. But why does he have to say it in a monkey suit?"

"Ohmi—Forget it. Men are so alike," she muttered, and looked out her window.

"Oh, and women aren't?" he asked. "And by the way, while you were convincing your friend with cold feet to go ahead and take the plunge, you were not navigating. The sign we just passed said Tyler. Would you please look and tell me how far to Tyler?"

"Tyler?" she repeated, and dug out the map. She studied it a moment, then glanced at him. "We're going the wrong way."

"Wrong way!" he said disbelievingly.

"We should be going south, not east."

Joe slapped his hand against the wheel. "Holy—"

"You were supposed to get on 45. Why didn't you get on 45? The sign said Houston; I don't know how you missed it."

"I wasn't the only one who missed it! You said left."

"Did I?" she said breezily.

Joe sighed and began to look for an exit to turn around.

They found their way onto Interstate 45… along with a million other people who probably had the same idea to catch a flight out of Houston. But at least they were moving. Joe checked the clock. It was almost three. If they could make it by six, they had a decent chance of getting out tonight, before the strike—

"I need a bathroom," Kate said.

"Oh my god," Joe muttered. "I thought you went at McDonald's."

"I did! I have a small bladder." She smiled sunnily, as if she were proud of it.

This was going to be the longest drive of his life, Joe thought. No contest. He took the next exit.

Chapter 4

WHEN KATE EMERGED FROM THE BATHROOM AT the Shell station, she felt sticky. It was overcast, warm, and very humid, which made it difficult to believe that a blizzard was engulfing half the country.

Joe was leaning against the front bumper. He'd removed his tie and stripped down to shirtsleeves, which he'd rolled up. His arms were crossed over his chest, and his biceps, Kate could not help noticing, were bulging against the fabric of his shirt. What did he do, spend every spare minute in a gym?

If a girl was going to be caught up in a catastrophe, it didn't hurt to be caught up with a guy as handsome as Joe… Somebody. Even if he did exhibit some Typical Male-ish tendencies from time to time.

But he looked good with his dark hair and blue eyes, and Kate, out of habit, smiled at him. Joe seemed surprised by her smile for some reason, and his gaze flicked over her face… lingering a moment too long on her mouth. "All better?" he asked.

"Much. Are you ready?"

"Baby, I was ready an hour ago," he said casually, and pushed off the bumper of the rental car.

"I'm just going to move my bag first," Kate said as she walked to the passenger side of the car. "There's not enough room for me and this."

She reached down to the floorboard and attempted to lift the bag with two hands, but it was wedged in.

"Here, I'll get it."

She hadn't heard Joe come up behind her and abruptly straightened up and twisted about, knocking into him when she did. Yep. His body was as hard as a turtle shell, just like she'd guessed. She blinked up at him as he reached around her and lifted the bag out. He tossed it onto the floor behind the front passenger seat. "What is in that thing, anyway?" he asked as he walked around the back of the car to the driver's side.

"Work," she said, sliding into the passenger seat.

Joe started the car. "What kind of work?"

"I am an editor," Kate said proudly. "Well, assistant editor," she amended. "But on track to be a full editor."

"What, like books?"

No, like nursery rhymes. "Yes. Like books."

He glanced at her and smiled wryly. "You don't have to say it like I am one step above a cow on the food chain."

"I didn't say it like you were one step above a cow," she said pertly, although she was aware that she had.

"What kind of books?" he asked.

Kate sat a little straighter in her seat as he pulled out of the parking lot. "Women's fiction."

"Women's fiction," he repeated carefully. "Would that be fiction about women?"

"It's fiction about relationships. And love. That sort of thing."

Joe gave her a dubious look. "You mean romance novels," he said, as if he'd just figured out a complicated puzzle. "What do they call them? Bodice rippers." He laughed.

"First of all, they are not only romance, and secondly, that is so ignorant," Kate said. "It's a cliché, and you wouldn't say it if you actually bothered to read one."

"What makes you think I haven't read one?"

"*Have* you?" she demanded.

"No!" he said with a laugh as if that was ridiculous. "I don't *read,*" he added. "I mean, tech manuals, yes. But not *books.*" He laughed again as if the mere suggestion was ludicrous. "Especially not books about relationships. I'd rather watch sports."

"Do you know how primitive you sound right now?" Kate said.

"Why? Because I would rather watch sports than read about other people having sex?" He winked at her. "See, I don't need to read about it."

Kate rolled her eyes. "And what do *you* do, Mr. Never Cracked a Book?"

"Hey, I take issue with that," he said with playful bravado. "I've cracked a few books in my time. I'm in technology, which—and this may surprise you—actually requires a fairly high level of reading comprehension. I create security systems for banks."

"*Knew* it," Kate said pertly.

"Knew what?"

"That you were probably in something like technology."

"What's that mean?" he asked. "Why did you think that?"

He looked so genuinely surprised that Kate couldn't help but laugh. "Because you're like an IT guy. You know."

"No, I do *not* know," he said waspishly. "I do not fit the stereotype, and frankly, I don't know anyone in my field who does."

"So now you are offended by stereotypes?" Kate laughed. "That figures."

"What figures?"

"You don't like stereotypes. And I'm saying not all romance books fit the stereotype of bodice ripper, either."

Joe grinned. "Okay. Touché. I won't judge a bodice ripper by its cover until I read one. Who knows? It could happen."

Kate laughed. "No, it couldn't."

Joe grinned, too—a warm, charming smile—and winked at her. "You're probably right. But I will reserve judgment just the same."

"Thank you," she said graciously.

"So tell me something, Kate. What is it about IT guys that get such a bad rap? I think we're kind of fun, actually."

Kate didn't get the chance to answer—her phone beeped. She picked it up and read the text message:

Mom says air controller strike. Maybe good reason to call it off?

"What is the *matter* with her?" Kate demanded of no one, and dialed Lisa's number.

"I knew you'd call," Lisa said somberly.

"What the hell, Lisa?" Kate said sternly. "Why

are you suddenly so unsure of everything? Just two weeks ago you were telling me that Kiefer was the best thing that ever happened to you. Are you going to tell me that now, after four years, in the space of two weeks he has gone from perfect to you wanting to call it off?"

"No! Sort of," Lisa moaned. "I don't know, Kate—I just have this bad feeling that he doesn't really want to marry me."

"Why? Why why why?" Kate asked angrily.

"Okay, like the other day," Lisa said. "I was trying to get him to help me with the drink menu for the rehearsal dinner. I mean, it's *his* responsibility, but do you think he has taken charge? *Nooo.* So I said, okay, this has to get done, and I sat down with him, and I said, 'I'm going to help you, but we have to decide what we are serving. Do you like wine?' And he was like, 'I guess,' and I said, 'Okay, what about liquor? Are we serving liquor? Because I don't want everyone getting wasted before my wedding day, which means you, by the way—'"

"*Me?*" Kate exclaimed.

"No, no, not *you.* Kiefer. I said that to Kiefer, because you know how he is, Kate. You know. So anyway, he wouldn't make any decisions at all and he finally said, 'Why don't *you* do it, Lisa? You've made up your mind.' I mean, he was *totally* abdicating to me, like he has the whole way with this wedding. He wouldn't help me decide about the church, or the flowers, or how big or small the guest list was. He just tells me to do it and then goes off and watches basketball. What does that say to you? It says to me he doesn't really want to get married."

"Wow," Kate said. "Yes, I agree he could be just a little more supportive of you. After all, this is his wedding, too," she said. "But it sounds to me like he's just being childish about it, and not that he doesn't want to marry you. If he didn't want to marry you, he's the kind of guy who would tell you, don't you think?" Kate looked to Joe for confirmation. He gave her an affirmative nod.

"I don't know," Lisa said.

"Well, I do. You're overreacting. Just relax. Pick the drinks for the rehearsal dinner. Tell Kiefer you guys need to talk about things—"

Joe suddenly shook his head, quite adamantly.

"But later. Much later," Kate added, and Joe nodded. "Right now, just focus on the wedding and how long you've been planning it, and how gorgeous you are going to be."

That seemed to appease Lisa. "You're right. It is going to be beautiful, isn't it? And I am going to be gorgeous. Did you just love the centerpieces? I can't wait to see you in that dress, Kate."

Kate rolled her eyes heavenward.

"Just be careful with it. That taffeta really wrinkles."

"I know," Kate said patiently.

"So when is your flight out?"

"Ah…" Kate quickly debated telling Lisa the truth. She rubbed the nape of her neck. "I'm not sure yet. They are rerouting a lot of people. But I'll let you know. So listen, I have to run—"

"I just hope you get out before the air traffic controller strike, because that is the *last* thing I need to deal with," Lisa said. "I *cannot* be without my maid of honor. I'd just as soon reschedule."

Lord. "You won't have to do that," Kate said as confidently as she could manage. "Do you still have that spa package I gave you? Did you schedule that massage?"

"No. But that is a great idea," Lisa said absently. "Yeah, I think I'll do that."

"Great. So listen, I better see about this flight. I'll call you later?"

She said good-bye and looked at Joe.

"See about what flight?"

"Trust me, it was the right thing to do," Kate said with a flick of her wrist. "Why are guys so damned insensitive?"

"Why are women so damned sensitive?" he easily countered. "What is it now?"

"Kiefer—that's my cousin's fiancé—is not help-ing," Kate said, and related the story of Lisa and Kiefer to Joe, from how long they'd been together, to Kiefer's grand proposal with Christmas lights and a high school chorus, to the last-minute wed-ding jitters and unwillingness to help.

Joe listened with a frown of concentration. When she'd finished, he said, "Wow."

"I know, right?" Kate said. "He's really being a jerk."

"I was thinking she was the jerk," Joe said.

Kate blinked. "*Lisa?* Lisa is doing everything!"

"And that's your problem right there," Joe said. "She's so caught up in this wedding and it being perfect that she isn't letting him do anything. He doesn't have any ownership in it. It's like he's been cut out."

"That's what I think—he's being childish."

"I didn't say that," Joe said. "I think he's just being a guy."

"A guy," she repeated with a bit of derision in her voice.

"Yes. A *guy*," he repeated firmly.

"So… you don't think he's having second thoughts?"

"Nah," Joe scoffed. "First of all, he wouldn't have asked her to marry him if he didn't love her.

Second, he is doing what he thinks he should be doing—giving her everything he thinks she wants. If he didn't want in, he would say so."

That almost made sense to Kate. "You sound like you've been down this path before."

"Me?" He laughed. "Hardly. But my brother has. Twice to be exact, and both women were totally eaten up with the wedding instead of the marriage."

Kate scarcely heard the last bit. She was focused on the *hardly*. "Why do you say it that way?" she asked him.

"Say what?"

"*Hardly*. You said hardly, like it was so out of the realm of possibility for you. Are you opposed to marriage?"

He gave her a bemused smile. "How on earth did you get that from what I just said? I'm not opposed to marriage. I don't think it's for me, but I'm not opposed to it."

"Why not?" she asked curiously. It was funny, but she'd had the same feeling about herself.

"I don't know," he said with a shrug. "I guess I've just never felt like I wanted to spend the rest of my waking days with one person."

"A guy like you?" she asked disbelievingly. She would think he'd have his pick of women.

"Who, an IT nerd?" he asked with a chuckle.

"No. A handsome man. A gentleman. I would think you had lots of girlfriends."

"Handsome, huh?" He grinned. "Yeah, I've had a few girlfriends along the way."

"But not one that you felt that way about."

"No," he said, and looked at her curiously. "Why? Is that so strange?"

Something about that made Kate feel a little uncomfortable, but she wasn't certain why. "Maybe you're too busy partying," she said.

"What?" Joe laughed. "Where did that come from?"

"Because this morning, you smelled slightly of alcohol. And you looked really hungover."

Joe's eyes widened with surprise.

"Dark circles, your hair messed up—"

"Okay, okay," he said, and laughed. "So maybe I had a few too many last night. But it's not what you think, kiddo. I happened to be the person of honor at a going-away party."

"Really?" she said, doubly curious now. "Why? Where are you going?"

"Seattle, remember?" He grinned at her. "I'm on my way to a new job. The kind of job that comes around once in a lifetime."

"Congratulations!" she said, and ignored the tiny niggle of disappointment she felt.

"Thanks." He smiled happily. "So what about you?"

"I'm from Seattle. But now I live in New York."

"No, I mean the marriage thing. Have you ever gotten close?"

"Umm… no," she admitted. "Never."

"Okay. That's surprising, too."

Kate could feel herself blushing. "Not really."

"Yes it is. You're very pretty," he said, and Kate felt the heat began to creep into her cheeks. "And you're smart. And, bonus points, you're a trouper."

"I am?" she asked, absurdly pleased by that compliment.

"So far," he said laughingly. "So why hasn't someone snatched you up?"

"Oh, come on—"

"No, really," he said. "I can't tell you how many women I meet who can't hang. Or maybe they can hang, but they can't *talk*." He shook his head. "It's disappointing, you know? You take a woman out to dinner, and she's hot, and then you discover she can't carry on an intelligent conversation."

"Are you kidding?" Kate asked. "What about being on the other side of the table? How many guys have I gone out with and then found out they are unread and uninterested in anything but sports scores?" She realized she'd just described what she knew of him and looked at him in horror.

But Joe laughed. "Touché, madam, touché. But you haven't answered the question. Why haven't you settled down?"

Kate smiled wryly. "I guess because I never felt that way about anyone, either. But unlike you, I didn't have a string of boyfriends to choose from."

"Now that's just too hard to believe," Joe said. "I'd think there'd be a line around the block, your poor navigation skills notwithstanding."

Kate laughed softly, but her cheeks were burning with self-consciousness. And pleasure. "At least I'm not an armrest hog," she said.

"Oh no, you're not going to pin that on me," Joe laughed. "*You* are *horrible* with the armrest."

"Everyone knows the middle seat gets the armrest!"

"I have never heard anything so ridiculous in my life," he scoffed. "You've got some wacky ideas floating behind those pretty green eyes, Kate."

She couldn't help it—she laughed.

"So how do you become an assistant editor?" he asked.

"You read a lot. And majoring in English helped. How do you become an IT guy?"

"You start by taking computers apart to see if you can put them back together."

Kate could picture a mop-top boy doing just that. "What is it about boys, always wanting to take things apart?"

"Sexist," he playfully accused her. "My sister is the one who showed me how. Why do girls always read a lot?"

"It's in our DNA. It so happens that there are more women book lovers than men."

"Include more sports scores and more men would read," he offered, smiling at Kate's laughter. "But the real question is, how do we get more women to deconstruct computers?"

"Good question," Kate said. "Computers are like cars. They should just work. No one wants to know how."

For the remainder of the drive to Houston, they argued playfully about the differences between men and women, and about who had the wherewithal to get to Seattle first.

As they entered the outskirts of Houston, rain began to fall. By the time they made their way across town to Houston's Intercontinental Airport, the rain had turned into a deluge. "You don't think this rain will delay flights even more, do you?" Kate asked, peering up at the sky as they dropped the rental car off.

"No, not at all," Joe said with a roll of his eyes. He grabbed Kate's bags.

"You don't have to do that," she said.

"I know," he said with a wink. "Come on, get that pink life raft and let's go find a flight out of here."

They crowded onto the shuttle, Kate with the garment bag on her back, Joe with her shoulder bag slung over his shoulder and cases in each hand. They ignored the looks of everyone who eyed her pink bag with disdain, then piled into the terminal with everyone else.

And into pandemonium.

"What the hell?" Joe said absently as they looked around.

A man standing just in front of them turned around. "The air traffic controllers just went on strike," he said.

Chapter 5

"We have to get that car back," Kate said instantly, crowding into Joe's side as a melee of angry, disgruntled passengers pushed and shoved toward the ticket counters. Joe couldn't help himself; he put a protective arm around Kate.

"We know what's going to happen," she said frantically. "Once they figure out they can't fly out, they will try and drive out, like us." She suddenly twisted into Joe's chest and grabbed his lapel, her green eyes wild. "We have to *go*."

"We can't drive out of this," Joe said, putting a hand on her arm. "It's at least a two-day drive in the best of weather, and we'd be driving into a blizzard."

Kate's grip tightened. "I think I am going to pass out."

"No, you're not," he evenly assured her, and gave her a comforting squeeze on the arm. "What about a train?"

"Train?"

"Yes, train," Joe said again, and gently peeled free the fingers clawed around his lapel so he could reach his cell phone. "If we can just get farther west, we have more options for getting to Seattle." At least he hoped that was true. He googled the Amtrak schedules and squinted at the screen. "Okay, we can book a ticket right now, leaving in a couple of hours, and arriving in Phoenix at 6:30 tomorrow night."

"Tomorrow!" Kate exclaimed, and did a dramatic little backward bend. "But that's the dress rehearsal! I'll miss the dress rehearsal, and I bought a gorgeous new dress to counter the peach thing!"

Joe looked up from his phone. "Do you know any other way to get there?"

Kate sighed with resignation. She looked down and shook her head. Tendrils of hair shook loose from the knot she'd tied in her hair earlier, and Joe had an insanely stupid urge to touch them, brush them back behind her ear.

"Listen, the important thing is that you get there in time for the wedding, right? And for me, Monday morning. I have to be there by Monday." He googled the location of the train station, then looked at Kate. "Should I buy the tickets?"

"*Yes*," she said, and punched him lightly in the chest for emphasis.

As it turned out, getting the tickets was the easy part. Getting across town looked impossible. The taxi stands were swimming with humans trying to leave the airport.

After twenty minutes of waiting, Joe was getting a little panicky himself. He'd been to Houston only a couple of times, but what he remembered was that it was huge and sprawling. He imagined that sprawl would seem to double in a rainstorm. "If we can't get in a cab soon, we won't make it," he said grimly.

"We're going to make it," Kate said, her determination returned.

"I don't think so," Joe said, looking at his watch.

"Okay, that's it," Kate said, and thrust the pink garment bag at him. "Hold this for me, please."

"Wait—where are you going?" he called after her, but Kate was marching up the line, her hips moving enticingly in the pencil skirt she was wearing. As her fair head disappeared into the crowd of people, he lost sight of her altogether.

Several minutes passed. Joe kept looking at his watch, wondering if he should go after her or stay put. When he looked up from his watch for what seemed like the hundredth time, he saw her walking back. But she was not alone—a porter with a red cart was walking alongside her.

And Kate was crying.

Joe's pulse instantly leapt. "Kate!" he shouted. His instinct was to go to her, but he had a stronger instinct to keep their place in line. "Kate, what's wrong?" he demanded as she walked up to him, her face streaked with the path of her tears. It alarmed him so that he grabbed her arms. "What happened? Are you all right?"

"Joe, it's *Dad*," she exclaimed, sniffling up at him as the porter stood uncomfortably to the side. "He's taken a turn for the worse. I got the call when I went to check on how long it would be."

"What?" Joe asked, confused. "Your dad?"

She suddenly grabbed his upper arms and squeezed so tight it was almost painful. "Joe," she said, her eyes narrowing just slightly. "I know you thought we'd make it on time, but unless we make that train, I won't see him again!" She burst into tears and buried her face in Joe's chest.

"Oh, the poor thing," a woman behind him said.

"Oh my god," Joe said. He was fairly certain there was no father issue and that Kate was working some mysterious, probably nonsensical angle, but then again, he didn't really know her. He couldn't be sure. He put his hand on the back of Kate's head, held her close to him. "I'm so *sorry*."

"Don't worry—one of our private car passengers

is going to give you a ride," the porter said, and gestured at Kate. "So she doesn't have to wait for a cab," he added in a loud whisper. "Are these your bags here?"

"What?"

Kate groaned and squeezed his arms again. Quite tightly. And then she grasped a bit of his coat fabric and gave it a tug. Wow. She'd found them a *ride*? He would take back every thought he'd just had about this being nonsense.

"Young man, he is asking if these are your bags," the kindly woman said behind him.

"Oh. Yes. Those," Joe said.

"Listen, you need to pull yourself together and help her," the woman continued, and patted his back. "She needs to say good-bye to her father. Now go take advantage of the offer and get to the train station before it's too late."

"Right," Joe said. "Thank you." To the porter he said, "Don't forget the pink thing." He put his arm around Kate's shoulders and pulled her tightly into his side. "Be strong, baby," he said. "We have to be strong for Dad." What was that he saw, the barest hint of a smile?

"I just need him to hang on a little longer," she said tearfully. "Why now?" she sobbed as they followed the porter to a black town car. "It's so unfair!"

Joe squeezed her tight in a silent plea not to overdo it.

In the backseat of the town car sat a woman in an expensive suit with a Louis Vuitton briefcase at her feet. She smiled sympathetically at Joe. "I'm so sorry," she said softly to Joe as he climbed in behind a limp Kate. "She is obviously very close to her father."

"So close," Joe said.

"It's so unexpected," Kate said through her tears.

"Right," Joe said, smiling ruefully at their benefactor as he tucked Kate into his body. "We can't thank you enough for the ride—she's a basket case."

Kate poked him in the side.

"I'm just so glad I can help." The woman leaned forward a bit to look at Kate, whose hair, thankfully, covered her face. Kate shuddered and made a sort of garbled sobbing noise. The woman eased back, glanced over Kate's head, and gave Joe a look brimming with sympathy.

As the car started slipping into traffic, Joe very slyly gave Kate a slight fist bump.

By the time they reached the train station, Kate had feigned a slight recovery. She was still tucked into Joe's side, which, he had to admit, he liked. She felt good next to him. All warm and soft. She was speaking somberly to the woman beside her, telling her what a great dad her father was. "Of all the times this would happen," she sighed. "The blizzard, the strike…"

"It's horrible," the woman agreed. "It took me two days to come home from London due to all the cancellations. I'm just glad I don't have to go any farther." The car coasted to a stop in front of the train station. "I wish you both the best of luck," she said. "Take care of yourself, Kate."

"Thank you. I will." Kate teared up again, and she took the woman's hands in both of hers. "Thank you so much."

Joe said his thanks, too, but hopped out as soon as he could and raced the driver to the trunk. The less pink the Good Samaritan saw, the better. He didn't want to her to be reminded of a wedding and start putting two and two together. He watched Kate come out of the town car, watched her bend over and wave, then stand there as the town car pulled away.

"Well played," Joe said. "Where did you learn to *cry* like that?"

"Drama club, Garfield High," Kate said morosely, then twirled around, arms wide. "God, what have I done, Joe? I just *lied* to that poor woman to get to the front of the line! What has *happened* to me? I don't lie to get my way! But look, the first sign of adversity and I am lying and crying and becoming someone I don't even recognize!"

"It's called survival," Joe said.

"I never felt so greasy in all my life," she said, running her palms down her thighs. "I'm a horrible person."

"Take it easy, Kate," Joe said and unthinkingly smoothed her hair back from her brow. "Ask yourself this: Would you rather lie to a complete stranger? Or call Lisa and tell her you can't make her wedding?"

Big green eyes blinked up at him and something shiny flashed in them. Kate grabbed her shoulder bag. "Come on, we have a train to catch." She swung her bag over her shoulder, hoisted the garment bag onto her back, and stalked toward the entrance.

You had to admire a woman like that, Joe thought. And he did. More than he would have ever expected upon first seeing her. Definitely way more than he wanted to.

—⁓—

It should not have come as a surprise that squeezing onto the overcrowded train was a bit like squeezing into the proverbial sardine can. Joe and

Kate scarcely made it on time, and as it took longer than normal to maneuver the pink raft through the cars, they could not find seats together. Joe sat two rows back from Kate. All he could see of her was the edge of the pink garment bag that she held on her lap. The bottom of it stuck out into the aisle, and he winced every time someone walked by and stepped on it.

Joe dozed on and off as the train trundled along, rocking gently side to side. Somewhere in the night he was rudely awakened by the harsh whisper of his name. When he opened his eyes, he saw only pink plastic, and then felt the pressure of a knobby knee on his thigh.

"Ouch!" he said as Kate half crawled, half fell over him into the seat next to him. He had no idea what had happened to the young woman sitting beside him. He had not seen her or felt her move over him to leave.

Kate landed with a thud.

"What time is it?" Joe asked with a yawn.

"Two," Kate said, and dragged the garment bag across their bodies, stuffing it into the space between her and the window. Apparently, she'd given up on trying to keep the dress wrinkle free. She dug in her shoulder bag and handed him a prewrapped sandwich.

"What's this?"

"Supper," she said. "I got them from the dining car before they closed. I hope you like tuna."

Joe did like tuna—from his kitchen. He was entirely suspicious of a prewrapped tuna sandwich from an Amtrak dining car. But then again, he was starving, and desperate times called for desperate measures.

Kate reached in her bag again and produced two cans of iced tea—another cause for gag reflex—and the pièce de résistance, a carefully wrapped chocolate-chip cookie that was the size of a small dinner plate. "Last one," she said proudly, and placed it on her lap, then unwrapped her tuna sandwich.

They both took a bite, chewing carefully. "May I ask you something?" she asked before taking another bite of a sandwich that looked just as soggy as his.

"Sure," Joe said.

"Do you believe in fate?"

Joe almost choked on the tuna. Generally, when a woman asked him if he believed in fate, it was the lead-in to a conversation about feelings. Joe did not like to talk about feelings. Most of the time he didn't even like to acknowledge he had them. Feelings, especially where women were concerned, were never clear-cut for him. They were messy and sticky, and he never seemed to say or feel the right thing.

He looked at Kate, who was making nice work of a disgusting tuna sandwich. She didn't really strike him as the kind of woman who wanted to discuss feelings, either. "Why do you ask? Do you?" he asked.

"I don't know," she said, and glanced at the window. There was nothing but black out there—they were passing through desert. "Most of the time, I'd say no. But today has been kind of weird. It almost feels like this was supposed to happen."

"What was supposed to happen?" he asked carefully.

"Me having such a difficult time getting to Seattle," she said, and Joe felt a rush of relief. "I mean, Lisa is teetering on the edge, and I am the only one who can get through to her. So I have to wonder, all these obstacles…" She looked at Joe and shrugged. "If, for some stupid reason, Lisa canceled the wedding, it's possible it's fate, right?"

Joe didn't know Lisa, but having listened in on two conversations, he figured it was more likely that Lisa was just a nut. "I think it would be more of a coincidence."

"Don't look at me like that," Kate said with a wry smile. "I may sound like a loon, but I'm not really. I've just been sitting on a train for the last few hours with nothing to do but think."

"I wasn't thinking you were crazy, Kate. I was just looking at you." He liked looking at her. She had some really expressive eyes, and he liked the way her nose was slightly upturned. And her mouth—hell, her *mouth*.

Joe made himself look at his sandwich. He wanted to kiss her. Just... *kiss* her.

"So, do you?" she asked.

"Pardon?" he asked with a small cough.

"Believe in fate."

"Ah..." He risked a look at her again. "Depends," he said noncommittally.

"Right," she said, nodding as if they'd just exchanged some meaningful ideas. "For me, too."

But Joe was thinking only about sex at the moment, imagining that mouth and those eyes beneath him. He looked away to give himself a good and silent talking-to. Thinking about sex wasn't going to help anything. It wasn't going to get them to Seattle, and it would only complicate this fragile, weird alliance they'd formed.

But he couldn't stop thinking about it at two in the morning on a train crossing the desert.

"I'm so *tired*," Kate said, and put down what was left of her sandwich. She leaned back and closed her eyes. "You can have the cookie," she said through a yawn.

Joe smiled. He gazed at her, wondering how he could have missed just how pretty she was when she knocked into him this morning in New York with the pink raft. Was that really just this morning? He felt as if he'd known her a lot longer than that.

He silently admired her features, right up to the moment her head slid down on his shoulder and she began to snore.

Chapter 6

LISA TOOK THE NEWS ABOUT KATE'S DELAY WITH a lot of whining, wailing, and "How am I going to *do* this without you?"

Kate talked her neurotic cousin off the ledge. She made her understand that she was only missing a dinner, not a major event. It was one meal. Not a huge loss—besides the dress, it was not even a small loss. Lisa said she understood. She even seemed to agree with Kate.

But not fifteen minutes after Kate had hung up, her mother called.

"When are you going to be here?" her mother demanded with a slightly accusatory tone.

"Mom, seriously. I am on a *train* to Phoenix. A train! I started on a plane, then a car, and now I am on a TRAIN. I am doing the best I can."

"Well, I didn't say you weren't," her mother sniffed. "It just seems like you could have rented a car or something."

"Mom, do you know where Texas is? It is very far away from Seattle. You can't drive from Texas to Washington in a blizzard!"

She must have been speaking with agitation, because Joe put his broad hand on her knee and squeezed reassuringly.

"Oh, I know," her mother said wearily. "I was just hoping. We'll all be sick if you miss the wedding, and Lisa doesn't need any distractions. I've always said that girl is too high strung for her own good."

"I won't miss the wedding," Kate said firmly. "We are almost to Phoenix, and we hear they are bringing scabs in."

"Bringing *what*?"

"Scabs."

"Strikebreakers," Joe offered. He had removed his coat again and loosened his collar. His hair, thick and dark brown, looked as if he'd dragged his fingers through it a dozen times. And he had a very sexy shadow of a beard that Kate had to tell herself not to stare at.

"Who is that?" her mother demanded, jarring Kate back to the present.

"Ah… Joe."

"Joe! Who's Joe?"

"He was on my flight. We're both trying to get to Seattle."

"Oh. You should invite him to the wedding," her mother said cheerfully, as if Kate and Joe were sitting in a café sipping mimosas. She'd never heard of Joe until this moment and was inviting him to a major family event. Her family was crazy.

"Oh my god," her mother said suddenly. "Here comes your aunt. I wonder what the crisis is *now,*" she muttered irritably. "You'd think Lisa was the first woman to ever get married. Katie, sweetheart, keep us posted. We'll hold the wedding for you if necessary!"

"Mom, you can't hold the wedding," Kate said, but her mother had already signed off.

Kate clicked off, made a sound of severe frustration, and Joe laughed.

"Your family sounds as crazy as mine."

"I think I've got you beat," Kate said. "Where is your family, anyway?"

"Scattered," he said. "My brother is in Paris—"

"Paris!"

"Married to a Frenchwoman. My dad and sister are in Connecticut and my mom in Illinois. Yours?"

"All in Seattle," Kate said. "My aunt and uncle— Lisa's parents—live right around the corner. It's like some weird religious-sect compound, everyone always back and forth." Joe laughed, but he had no idea how tied up in each other's business they all were.

"So while you were assuring your mother you're not just playing hooky, I was digging for news. It looks as if the major airports, like Phoenix, will have enough controllers to get a few flights off the ground."

Kate gasped. "Really? You mean we might really get to Seattle?"

"If we can book a flight," he said. "I'm going to make a call. I've got a kick-ass travel agent."

He punched in the number and then said, "Hey, Brenda. It's Joe." And he smiled. It was a very easy, very sexy smile, and Kate imagined it could melt the false eyelashes off a woman. "Remember that trip we booked to Seattle? Well, I've run into a little trouble…"

Fifteen minutes later, Kate sat with her arms folded tightly across her, mildly annoyed at the number of times Joe chuckled. If he was going to book a flight, she didn't see why he didn't just *book* it instead of chatting on and on with Brenda, whoever she was, who was probably old enough to be his mother.

"Okay, we'll book Kate onto that flight," he said. "Hold on." He covered his phone. "What's your last name, anyway?"

"Preston."

"Preston," he said into the phone. "Just put it on my account. And yeah, I'll take the next one."

"What next one? You're not flying with me?" Kate asked.

Joe grabbed her hand and wrapped his fingers around hers, holding it against his rock-hard thigh. "Great. Thanks, Brenda. I owe you those Maroon 5 tickets."

Rats. Maroon 5 was not a grandma band.

Joe clicked off and beamed at Kate, squeezing her hand. "You're booked on the last seat of that flight tonight, Kate Preston."

She gasped. "Are you kidding?"

"Would I kid about something like that? Yes, for real."

"What about you?"

"I'm going tomorrow. But I don't have to be there until Monday. You needed to be there yesterday."

He was smiling. He was happy to have arranged it. Kate made herself smile. "Thank you. I owe you. Again."

"Not to worry," he said. He looked at her strangely. "What's the matter? I thought you'd be happy."

"I *am*," she said, nodding adamantly. "I just…" *Really like you. Sorta don't want this to end. Want to write a sitcom about two people who meet on a plane…*

Kate looked away from his silvery blue eyes.

"You know what? I don't think that tuna-fish sandwich was a good idea."

He laughed. "It was a *horrible* idea. I'm going to book a hotel room. After that, I'll take you on in Words with Friends if you're up to it."

Kate jerked her gaze to him. "Oh, I'm up to it," she said, digging out her phone. "I am *so* up to it."

The hours, she was sad to note, flew by as they played Words with Friends until Joe lost juice in his phone. By that time, they were nearing the Phoenix station, slightly ahead of schedule. Joe had taken care of everything, including transport to the airport, and refused all of her efforts to repay him.

They arrived at the airport in a transport van— Joe, Kate, their bags, and a crumpled pink garment bag. Kate didn't have the heart to look at the bridesmaid dress now. She could see that one side of it wasn't as poufy as it had been starting out and shuddered to think what else had happened in there.

Joe got out with her, helped her with her bags. "So," he said, shoving his hands through his hair. "I guess this is it."

"I guess so," Kate said. She tried to smile. "I don't know your last name," she said.

"Firretti," he said.

"Firretti," she repeated, savoring the name a moment. "It sounds so…"

"Intelligent?" he offered.

Kate laughed. "I was going to say sporty."

Joe smiled.

"So… you're moving to Seattle."

"I am. And you're staying in New York."

"Yeah," she said softly.

Joe touched her cheek with his knuckle. "I have to say, although you suck at navigating, I can't imagine a better partner in this little jaunt across the country."

That made Kate feel warm and tingly all over. "And I should say that although you're a terrible armrest hog, I'm really glad you ended up next to me."

Joe stroked her cheek, touched her earlobe, then reluctantly dropped his hand. "Take care, Kate. Call me if you need anything."

"Okay… but your phone is dead."

"Right. I'm going to charge it at the airport Hilton," he said, jerking his thumb over his shoulder. "In about thirty minutes, it will be good to go. So, call me if something comes up."

"Okay," she said weakly. "You should call me, too. I can give you some tips about Seattle if you need them."

"I'll do that," he promised.

There was nothing left to say. Kate smiled ruefully.

Joe sighed, took her elbow in hand, and leaned forward to kiss her cheek. "Take care, Kate. But go now, or you'll miss your flight." He picked up her bag and put it on her shoulder.

"Thanks," she said. "Seriously, Joe Firretti, thanks for everything." She picked up the garment bag, pulled the stem of her suitcase. "Bye."

"Good-bye, Kate."

Kate started walking, moving through the glass doors into cool, slightly fetid air. When the doors closed behind her, she glanced back.

Joe was still standing there, watching her. He lifted his hand.

So did Kate. She smiled again, then turned away, walking on, feeling exhausted, a little queasy, and indescribably sad.

Chapter 7

THE AIRPORT HOTEL WAS A LITTLE DINGY, THE room furnishings a little worn, but the only thing Joe cared about was that it had a shower and a bed. After he'd washed the last thirty-six hours from his body, he pulled on some lounge pants and ordered a burger, fries, and a beer, and settled in to catch up on sports.

But his gaze kept shifting to the window, from which he would see the occasional planes the scabs managed to send out over the red mountains of Phoenix.

Joe was not particularly proud of it, but a few years ago, he had been a real dog when it came to women. That was how he'd met Brenda the Travel Agent. She was nice, but turned out to be a little vanilla for his tastes.

Fortunately, their short dating history had ended well, and the girl could work some travel magic.

He knew because part of his job had been to travel, and Brenda had always managed to get him home without much trouble. Uprisings, tsunamis, volcano ash, and terrorist threats were no match for her.

Joe was glad she'd gotten Kate into the last seat on the last flight out to Seattle. Glad in a non-doglike, adult way of doing something nice for someone for a change. So why was he hoping Kate hadn't made that plane? And what sort of dumbass was he for not asking to see her in Seattle? He'd thought about it—of course he had—but that thought had been followed by a bunch of other thoughts crowding in and stifling it, like *Why*, and *What's the point*, and *Get a grip, it's just a girl*.

Yeah. A girl. A really cool, really good-looking girl. A girl who had somehow managed to make him sit up and take notice like he hadn't done in a very long time.

Smooth, Firretti.

The sun was beginning to set, and Joe couldn't see the planes anymore. Kate had obviously made it—her flight would have departed a half hour ago, and she hadn't called. He closed his eyes and listened to the ESPN guy talk about the Phoenix Suns' chances this season.

A knock on the door brought him off the bed. "Thank God," he said. His stomach was growling.

He walked to the door and opened it, then stumbled back a step with surprise.

"I hope you don't mind," Kate said apologetically from just behind the pink raft.

"No," Joe said quickly. "You missed your flight?"

"Ah… rescheduled. First thing tomorrow." Kate winced and put a hand to her belly. "I wasn't feeling too well. Tuna fish, I think."

His grin was slow but broad. "That was some rank tuna fish," he agreed. "You'd better come in."

She smiled and pushed the pink raft at him. "Thanks!"

He wrestled the garment bag into the rack behind him, and when he turned back, Kate held up a six-pack of beer. "I thought beer would help my tummy," she said. "And you seem like a beer guy."

"I'm going to take that as a compliment," he said, grabbing her bags and pulling them in. "Where did you get that, anyway?"

"From the same guy who told me what room you're in," she said. "I have my ways."

"Don't tell me. I might be jealous." He grinned at her and stepped back to allow her entry. "By the way, just what does a beer guy look like?" he asked as she slipped past him.

Kate paused. Her gaze dropped to his bare chest,

to his lounge pants, and slowly rose again. "Like *that*," she said. Her voice had changed. "Just like that," she added quietly.

Joe could feel the draw between them, the unmistakable chemistry kicking up and swirling about them into a lethal mix of desire and admiration. It felt as if everything Joe had ever wanted in a woman was standing right in front of him—with too many clothes on, but still—and he was vaguely amazed he'd ever let her walk into that airport without him. He wanted to say all those things, but he felt strangely tongue-tied. He could only reach for her, and at the same moment, she leaped at him.

Joe crushed her to him, his mouth on her lips, as soft and lush as he'd imagined them to be. Kate grabbed his head between her hands and teased him with her tongue, plunging him into a familiar fog of arousal and desire. But this was different than the usual. This felt deeper and somehow more important.

He whirled her around and pushed her up against the door. Her warm, wet mouth was as tormenting to him as it was pleasurable. Her body curved into his, rattling him in every bone, in every nerve. He thrust his hands into her hair, moved his mouth to her neck.

He'd never felt anything as strongly as he was

feeling the need to be with Kate—beside her, around her, in her. He caressed her sides, her torso, her breasts, and Kate made a little groaning sigh into his mouth that sent him careening down a slope of yearning.

He whirled her around again, crashing into the rack that passed as a closet.

"Not the dress!" she whispered frantically against his cheek, and Joe whirled again, bumping into the mirror tacked to the wall. The thing came off and crashed behind Kate.

Joe suddenly threw his arms around her waist and lifted her up off her feet, falling onto the bed with her. He dipped down to the hollow of her throat, to the vee in her shirt, tasting her skin, feeling the faint beat of her heart, racing in time with his.

A pounding at the door made them both freeze. Kate stared wide-eyed at him.

"Burger," he muttered to her deliciously creamy breasts.

Kate gasped. "*Burger*," she repeated lustfully, and abruptly pushed him off her. She jumped up, buttoning her blouse as she hurried to the door. Joe groaned and fell face forward onto the bed. He heard her thanking whoever had brought it, assuring that person she had the tray under control. The door shut, and a moment later, Kate reappeared with the room service tray, her hair charmingly messed, her blouse only crookedly rebuttoned, and a french fry sticking out of the side of her mouth. She slid the tray onto the desk.

Joe grabbed her around the waist and pulled her back down onto the bed. "But I'm *starving*," Kate laughingly implored him.

"So am I," he growled, and began to kiss her neck as he unbuttoned her blouse again.

She sighed softly. Her hands were moving on him again, sweeping over his arms and hips. She dropped her head back with a gasp of pleasure as Joe sought more of her bare skin with his mouth. He felt like he had a rattlesnake under his skin, his body one mess of quivering, jangled nerves.

Kate pressed against the hard ridge of his erection and inhaled a ragged, ravenous breath. White-hot shivers of anticipation ran up Joe's spine. He rolled over, pulling her to straddle his lap. Kate cupped his face. Her gaze moved over his eyes, his nose, and his mouth. "Joe Firretti," she said softly, "where the hell did you come from?"

"I was wondering the same thing about you," he said, and pushed a golden lock back from her face. He kissed her softly, slid his hands to her shoulders, then her rib cage, and down, to her hips. He dipped a hand beneath the hem of her skirt and slid it up her thigh.

Kate's sigh was long and sweet. It reminded Joe of contentment, the sort of sound one might make when returning home, to the place they were meant to be. Her arms encircled his neck, and she kissed him back, slowly now, savoring it.

Joe found the zipper in her skirt and pulled it down, and somehow, between the two of them, she shimmied out of it. Her blouse had come completely undone, and underneath it she wore a lacy red bra that made his blood boil. He rolled again, putting Kate on her back, and moved his hand higher, touching the soft flesh of her inner thigh.

When his fingers brushed the apex of her legs, Kate reached for his lounge pants, her fingers finding the tie and undoing it, then pushing them down his hips, wrapping her fingers around him. Joe stroked her and Kate moved against his hand. She made a small cry of pleasure and Joe couldn't tolerate it another moment. He slid into her.

He began to move inside her, teetering on the edge of his own powerful climax, moving faster as Kate moved with him, her breath coming quicker and harder. Her fingers curled into his arms, and she suddenly lifted up, gasping with the sensation of her climax.

Joe couldn't contain himself; he flew apart and rained down in tiny bits of himself onto that bed.

Moments passed—blissful, satiated moments—before Kate cupped his face and smiled.

He smiled, too, could feel the satisfaction of that smile reaching deep into him. He gathered her in his arms and kissed her cheek, her hair, and her mouth once more before settling down with her tucked into his side. He could feel her lips curve into a smile against his chest, her fingers tracing a long and lazy line down his side.

"I am so glad you missed your flight," he said, still a little breathless.

"Me too," she agreed and giggled.

Chapter 8

SITTING ON THE BED, NUDE BUT FOR THE SHEET wrapped loosely about her, eating half of a man's burger and washing it down with his beer was the best post-coital experience Kate had ever had in her life.

She couldn't stop grinning. She'd never had sex like *that*, and it was a revelation to her. So many thoughts and feelings were fighting for recognition in her, bits and pieces of them scattering about in euphoria.

This, Kate thought, was what she wanted. This, right here, with this guy, Joe Firretti.

She grinned at him again. Joe didn't notice—he was too engrossed in the manuscript she was editing. He was propped up against a stack of pillows, the sheet covering him from the waist down. His brow was furrowed in concentration. Kate slipped her hand across his rock-hard abdomen, but Joe caught her wrist and squeezed lightly. "Stop that, you vixen," he said without looking up from the pages. "I have never used the word 'vixen' in my life until this moment. But I have to find out if she's going to let him in her house or not."

"Of course she does."

"Hey!" Joe protested, putting down the pages and casting a playfully stern frown at her. "Don't *tell* me. That ruins it."

Kate laughed. "If she doesn't let him in, there's no love story."

"Oh. I get it." He grinned and tossed the pages to the foot of the bed. "You're an expert, I take it," he said as he gathered her up in his arms. He kissed her, then snagged another fry. "Tell me what you like," he said.

"What I *like?*"

"Yes." He ate another fry. "What makes you happy? Puppies and ribbons? Rugby and scuba diving?"

Kate thought about that. "Shoes," she said with a definitive nod.

"I should have guessed that based on the weight of your suitcase alone. What else?"

This was what Kate was discovering she particularly liked about Joe. Yes, the sex was amazing, but better still, he was willing to talk. About everything. She tried to remember the last time she'd lounged on a bed—naked—and talked about sports and books and popular TV shows. She wondered if she'd ever known someone who would laugh with her about politics, or know the best sushi places in New York, or *agree* with her that Justin Bieber actually had put out a few catchy tunes.

Kate was not one for clichés. In the books she edited, she weeded them out and struck them from the pages. But at present she was wallowing in a cliché, because she truly, deeply felt as if she'd been waiting all her life for a guy like Joe Firretti to come around.

It sucked, it totally sucked that he was moving to Seattle. Fate—if such a thing existed—was playing the cruelest joke imaginable on her.

They watched Jimmy Kimmel, then took a shower together and made love again. Only slower. They took their time, learning each other, trying different things. And then they lay in the dark, Kate's head on his shoulder, their fingers laced together.

"Hey," Kate said. "Want to come to a wedding with me?"

Joe stroked her hair. "Do you promise to wear the mysterious pink-raft dress?"

She smiled in the dark. "If I haven't destroyed it."

"Then yes," Joe said, and kissed the top of her head. "I would like to go to a wedding with you."

"Assuming we make it," Kate said.

"Oh, we'll make it, baby," Joe said. "We haven't even touched the boat industry yet."

Kate laughed. "We really did have quite an adventure, didn't we?"

"That's an understatement."

"So... do you believe in fate yet?" she teased him.

She could hear Joe's soft chuckle. "You have to admit, it's wild that we met like we did and ended up here, just to say good-bye in a day or so."

"'Wild' is not the word that comes to my mind."

Hers either, really. She could see his blue eyes in the light from the window, shining into hers. "We make a good team, Joe Firretti."

"We make an *excellent* team," he agreed. "Minus the navigation."

"And the armrest issue," she reminded him.

He grinned.

"If you were still in New York, do you think we'd... I mean, would it be presumptuous to think that maybe—"

"Baby," he said, "we'd *definitely* be checking out some sushi bars and the Giants games, are you kidding?"

She smiled, kissed his chest. That made her a little sad, really. "When you come to visit, we can do that, right?"

"Right. And when you're in Seattle," he added.

Right. She didn't let the thought that she only made it to Seattle twice this year—this being the second time—linger. Maybe she'd come back more often. Maybe she'd make editor and get a raise and come back at least once a month. She refused to allow the reality of her situation to ruin the moment.

Maybe Joe was hearing the tinny voice of reality, too, because neither of them spoke after that.

Kate couldn't say when she drifted off to sleep, but she was awakened by an alarm that brought her off the bed. She pushed her hair from her eyes and looked around. Joe was standing at the foot of the bed, grinning at her. He had on a pair of jeans, a white collared shirt, and a blue blazer. "Rise and shine, kid. We don't want to miss that plane. Weather says a big storm is headed for Pacific coast."

As much as Kate wanted to extend her stay with Joe, the thought of being stuck in Phoenix did not appeal. She dug a pair of yoga pants from her bag, as well as a tank top and hoodie.

Against all odds, when Joe and Kate arrived at the airport, the pink raft in tow, their flight to Seattle showed an on-time departure. At the gate, Kate stood at the window, staring at the plane that had somehow managed to fly in from Los Angeles, and called Lisa, waking her to tell her she'd make it to the wedding.

"Oh thank God!" Lisa said with relief. "Mom!" she shouted. "MOM! Kate's going to make it!"

"So is everything okay?" Kate asked, as Joe appeared, two lattes in hand.

"Yes," Lisa said. "Why? What do you mean? Do you mean something?"

"No! But yesterday you were a little freaked out—"

"Pre-wedding jitters," Lisa said dismissively. Kate could hear her moving around, could hear water running. "Everyone says that's all it is."

Joe handed Kate a latte. She smiled at him. "So you're okay?" she asked again.

"Yes, I am okay," Lisa said, sounding like her normal self. "I mean, sure, Kiefer could have been slightly more supportive and all that, but I know that a guy like him only comes around once in a lifetime."

Kate lifted her gaze to Joe. He winked at her. "Tell me about it," she said. "By the way, I'm bringing someone to the wedding."

"Who?"

"The guy on my flight who helped me get across the country," Kate said. "His name is Joe Firretti."

"Yeah, bring him, bring him!" Lisa said excitedly. "Do you know that everything is shut down from Colorado east? It's a miracle you got as far as you did. We want to hug him!"

"No, please—"

"When are you getting in?"

"Ten this morning," Kate said.

She made arrangements with Lisa for someone to pick her up, then hung up and smiled a little tentatively at Joe. "They can't wait to meet you," she said.

"I can't wait to meet them," he said.

Yes, well, he might change his mind after the full force of the Prestons had been visited upon him.

Chapter 9

THEY WERE LUCKY TO BE ON THE SAME FLIGHT, Joe figured, even if they couldn't sit together. He could see just the top of Kate's head above a middle seat a few rows ahead of him and wondered if she'd begun her attack on the armrest yet. Every once in a while, she would sit up, turn around, and smile at him. She had happy eyes, he thought. Big, green, happy eyes. He wouldn't mind starting every day with big, green, happy eyes.

It seemed ridiculously unfair that Joe would meet a girl like Kate just as he was about to take the biggest step in his career. If he believed in fate, he would be calling it a few choice names right now.

They landed without a hitch in Seattle, but Joe could hear the guy behind him on the phone as they taxied to the gate. He was irate that the next leg of his flight had been canceled. Weather or air traffic, Joe didn't know. He was thankful he was at last where he needed to be. Disaster had been averted; he would meet the boss from Switzerland and begin his new job.

He didn't feel quite as excited about it as he had forty-eight hours ago.

Kate was waiting for him in the passenger ramp, the pink raft propped up beside her. She smiled brightly at him when she saw him and caught his hand. "Wait," she said as he tried to move forward, and pulled him to the side.

"What's wrong?"

"Okay," she said, "Listen. My family is tight. *Really* tight. So tight they can be a little overbearing," she said with a charming wince. "And I don't bring guys home a lot. Maybe never. So..." She shrugged.

Joe smiled at her angst. "Kate, it's okay," he said. "I can handle them." He picked up her garment bag, tossed it over his shoulder, and took her hand in his.

"So here we go," Kate said, looking down at their clasped hands as they made their way up the passenger ramp.

"Here we go, two people who have been brought together by an epic travel meltdown."

Kate smiled. But her smile didn't seem quite as bright as it had earlier this morning, when she'd been so deliciously naked in his bed. Families had a way of doing that to a person.

At the baggage claim area, the little scream of happiness Joe heard turned out to be for Kate. He turned just in time to see an older woman who looked like Kate barreling right toward them, a couple of guys and another woman with her.

"Oh thank God, you *made* it!" the woman shouted, and threw her arms around Kate, squeezing her tightly, weaving back and forth. Then she suddenly put Kate at arm's length. "Where's the *dress*?"

"Right there," Kate said, pointing at Joe. Joe wondered how anyone in Seattle could have missed the arrival of the dress. "Mom," Kate said, "this is Joe Firretti."

"And the dress," Joe added, holding up the pink raft.

"Oh, thank God again," the woman said, her shoulders dropping with relief.

"This is my mom, Sandra," Kate said. "And my dad, James. And my brother Colton and my sister Cassidy."

"With a C," the young woman said.

"Pleasure," he said to them all, and he was still smiling when Kate's mother moved. Joe thought she meant to take the dress from him. But instead, she threw her arms around him. "Thank you so much for bringing my baby home," she said, sounding almost tearful.

"He didn't bring me home," Kate said. "We were on the same flight, and we were both coming to Seattle."

"Don't try and downplay it, Katie-Kate," her mother said, beaming up at Joe. "We owe this young man a debt of gratitude."

"We'll pay him later, Sandra," Mr. Preston said, and clapped Joe on the shoulder as if they were old friends. "You didn't take any liberties with my little girl, did you, son?"

"Dad!" Kate cried, clearly mortified.

Mr. Preston squeezed Joe's shoulder and laughed. "Kidding! Come on, let's go. I told Glen I'd help him get the bar set up."

"And we have hair and makeup this afternoon," Mrs. Preston added. "Come on, Joe, we've made up a cot for you in the library."

"That's not necessary," he said quickly, holding up a hand. "I've got a reservation—"

"Nonsense!" Mrs. Preston said firmly. "You will come with us. We have plenty of room, and after what you did for Kate, I wouldn't have it any other way. Just call the hotel and tell them you'll be there tomorrow."

"What makes you think he did it all?" Kate asked. "It's not like we mushed across the country."

"Don't be a sourpuss," Mr. Preston said cheerfully, and grabbed her tote bag, handing it to Colton.

Kate looked helplessly at Joe. "See?"

He winked at her. He liked the Prestons. He liked them a lot.

———————

The Prestons lived in the Queen Anne district of Seattle, an area of old and well-loved homes. The Preston house was a rambling turn-of-the-century, five-bedroom, three-bath home with wood floors and dark window casings and a view of Lake Union. It was charming and a little quirky, just like Kate.

As they pulled into the drive, people rushed from the house, shouting for Kate, embracing her as she emerged. One would think she'd spent forty days in the desert instead of two days traveling across country.

She glanced back at him more than once, her expression apologetic. "They're nuts!" she insisted.

"They love you," he said as they were swept along on a wave into the house.

"Here, dude, a beer," someone said, shoving a bottle into his hand. It wasn't even noon. But Joe wasn't turning down a beer. He'd just taken a sip when he heard a woman shout from the top of the stairs. Everyone paused and looked up. *"Kaaaaate!"* the woman cried as she flew down the stairs.

The bride, Joe realized, had appeared.

She grabbed Kate, hopping up and down, babbling about backup maids of honor. "The *dress*," she said.

"In the car," Kate said quickly.

Why that should make the bride cry, Joe had no idea, but she burst into tears, and as he stood, dumbfounded, he watched Kate, Lisa, and little sister Cassidy with a C race upstairs.

"Get used to it," one man said to Joe. "This is the family you're marrying into."

"Not me," Joe said quickly.

The man squinted at him. "You're not Kiefer? Who are you, then?"

"Joe." At the man's blank look, Joe couldn't help but laugh. "I'm the guy who was sitting next to Kate when the plane was diverted to Dallas."

The man looked confused. "Huh?"

Joe grinned and took a swig of beer. It was going to be an interesting day. "Is there anything to eat?" he asked.

"Are you serious? J. J. made his ribs. You like ribs?"

"Love 'em," Joe said, and followed the man to the back of the house where he supposed he would find J. J. and his ribs.

———〰〰———

When Kate pulled the peach monstrosity from the bag, Lisa sank onto Cassidy's bed with a crushed expression. "It's *ruined*."

"No, no, not ruined," Kate said quickly. "Right, Cassidy? We can steam out these wrinkles, and the sash, well… maybe I just go without the sash."

"The sash makes the dress," Lisa said morosely.

"Okay. It's all okay, Lisa," Kate said, thinking frantically.

"What's *that*?" Cassidy asked, peering closely at the hem.

So did Kate. There was a yellowish, brownish stain that looked a little like mustard spreading across several inches of the hem. How had *that* happened?

"Oh my god!" Lisa cried.

"No one is going to see that!" Kate said, a little loudly. "And besides, everyone is going to be looking at you, anyway. It's *okay*!"

Lisa sniffed. She examined the wrinkled dress. One half was less poufy than the other. Lisa forced a smile. "At least *you're* here without weird stains, right? That's the important thing. Now I have all the people I love with me." She hugged Kate tightly for a moment. "And Joe is so *cute*!" she added as she let her go.

"He's gorgeous," Cassidy agreed. "Is he your boyfriend?"

"No!" Kate said instantly, and then flushed. As if that wasn't bad enough, she smiled nervously. She couldn't help it.

"What's that smile?" Lisa asked, poking her.

"No smile," Kate said, still smiling. "This is not a smile."

Lisa suddenly gasped and sank down on the bed. "Ohmigod, did you guys *do* it?"

"Lisa!" Kate cried and looked at her kid sister.

"Well, did you?" Cassidy demanded. "I mean, he's so cute, and you haven't had a boyfriend in forever."

"That," she said, pointing at Cassidy, "that is *not* true."

"You sure haven't had a *good* boyfriend," Lisa agreed. "And you obviously like Joe."

"Yeah," Kate said, her smile fading. "But he's moving to Seattle."

"No way!" Cassidy exclaimed.

"That's great!" Lisa said. "You can get a job

here! It would be so great if you came back! We miss you so much!"

"I can't come back, Lisa. I have always wanted to be in publishing, and I have a great job."

"Joe and Kiefer could be friends," Lisa continued.

"They haven't even met," Kate pointed out.

"But they will!" Lisa said excitedly. "I just want you to be as happy as I am, Katie-Kate. I want you to know what I feel for Kief."

Kate snorted. "Do you know how ridiculous you sound right now? Just *yesterday* you wanted to call it off."

"You *did*?" Cassidy asked.

"Not really," Lisa said with a flick of her wrist, as if yesterday had never happened. "I never would have done it because I love Kiefer too much. And I'm going to whip him into shape."

Kate and Cassidy laughed outright.

"Seriously," Lisa said, ignoring their laughter, "I know what a great guy Kiefer is. And it's like I told you: great guys come around once in a lifetime." She looked meaningfully at Kate.

That's what Kate was afraid of.

She was relieved when her mother burst into the room and had a fit over her dress. "Well, I have my work cut out for me this afternoon, don't I?" she sighed as she examined the sash. "In the meantime, you girls are going to be late to the hairdresser! Lori is outside waiting for you."

"What about Joe?" Kate asked as Cassidy and Lisa gathered their purses.

"Don't worry about him," her mother said as she busily inspected the gown. "He's out back with your father and your Uncle Glen looking at rototillers."

Kate gasped. "Mom, *no*!"

"He'll be fine! He looked really interested," her mother insisted, and began to herd them out the door. "Right now, you have bigger things to worry about. If we don't get Lisa married today, we may never have another opportunity."

"Hey!" Lisa protested, but Kate's mother had already pushed her out the door.

Chapter 10

THANKS TO THE GENEROUS NUMBER OF BATH-rooms and irons in the Preston house, Joe was able to clean up and shake out a suit to wear to the wedding. He hadn't seen Kate all day, but her mother would periodically pop in to give updates. "The girls are getting their hair done," she would say. "The girls are at the nail salon."

Seemed to Joe they spent more time on the hair and makeup and whatever else it was they were doing than the wedding itself. He didn't mind, though. He was suitably entertained by the Preston men—father, brother, cousins, and friends. First, there was the inspection of a broken rototiller. Next was a rousing debate about the possibilities of the Seattle Seahawks going All The Way next year. Joe had been in Seattle enough to be able to toss in a few thoughts about the NFL and the Seahawks, and as a result, was hailed as "a guy's guy."

Joe really liked these men. They were the sort of guys he would hang out with, go to games with, get a beer with. It would be something he could look forward to, if it weren't for one small problem: Kate would be leaving soon.

The situation with Kate was difficult to think about on such a festive day. They'd shared a really weird and fabulous few days, but how could it ever be anything more than something to regale his friends with in the years to come? It wasn't as if either of them would give up a job based on one long weekend. Joe thought he understood how these things went—you meet, you hook up, you go on with life. What other choice did he have? He'd allow himself a couple of days of moping about it, but what more could he do?

He told himself to have a good time tonight. Make it count. *And then go on with your life.*

He told himself that right up to the moment he saw Kate walking down the aisle in what was perhaps the ugliest dress he'd ever seen. It was a color not found in nature. It was wrinkled, and one half was less poufy than the other. But the remarkable thing about that dress was not how ugly it was, but how fantastic Kate made it look.

In a word, *wow*. She looked gorgeous with her hair swept up and ribbons cascading down her back. In spite of the condition of the dress, it fit her beautifully, hugging every curve. To Joe, Kate looked more beautiful than the bride, more beautiful than the flowers that adorned every pew and that altar. She was… everything. Everything that came to his mind when he thought of the perfect woman.

On the arm of some sad sack as she glided down the aisle, she caught sight of Joe and her face lit with a brilliant smile. Joe felt the warmth of that smile trickle down his spine, slide into his limbs, his fingers and toes, and warm his chest like an atomic glow.

He grinned back at her, and as she moved past, she gave him a subtle wink that made him as happy as a puppy. He was admiring her slender back as she walked by and almost missed the strange yellow-brown stain at the hem of the fluffy gown. And the wrinkled sash.

His smile went even deeper.

He didn't actually hear much of the ceremony, as his entire being was focused on Kate. He couldn't take his eyes from her.

Joe rode with Mr. Preston to the reception. It was in an industrial building, but the inside had been decorated to resemble what Joe guessed was a Southern plantation, with wispy sheers of silk draped overhead, a pergola dripping in fake

wisteria over the bridal table, and tall, skinny flo-
ral arrangements bursting with lilies and more silk
wisteria gracing the center of each table.

"Joe, over here!" Mrs. Preston called to him
from near the buffet. She had dressed in a shade
of peach for the occasion. "We've put you next to
Kate," she said, and leaned in next to him. "We had
to move Aunt Emily, but she'll be sleeping in her
soup anyway," she confided. She pointed to a seat
at the bridal table.

"I don't want to displace anyone," Joe said.

"Trust me, Aunt Emily will be happier sitting
with the Bergers. I don't know about them…" She
smiled. "Help yourself to champagne punch. The
bridal party should be here any moment."

Joe did as she suggested. He was chatting it up
with another of Kate's cousins when the bridal party
arrived, streaming in like peach-colored ribbons.

Joe watched as Kate stopped to greet people she
knew, hugging one or two tightly, laughing with
another. When she finally reached him, he handed
her a glass of champagne punch.

"Wow," she said, beaming up at him. "You look
so *nice,* Joe Firretti."

"And you, Kate Preston," he said, lifting his
glass, "are stunning."

"Oh, stop," she said with fake modesty, and

twirled around in the dress, almost knocking over a candelabra in the process. "What do you think?"

"I think," he said, looking down at the dress, "that it is the ugliest, most hideous, god-awful poufy piece of taffeta in the history of the world," he said, repeating the words she'd said to him in Dallas.

Kate burst out laughing.

"But I think it's hanging on one of the most gorgeous women I have ever seen."

Her smile was glowing. "*Thank* you," she said, curtsying. "You're just being nice." She touched her glass to his. "But I'm still going to memorize everything you just said and repeat it to myself several times a day."

"I mean it. You're beautiful," he said solemnly.

Kate's smile melted into something he understood. He was feeling the same regret and happiness, the same joy and sadness that he saw shimmering in her eyes.

Uncle Frank bumped into them at that moment and grabbed Kate up in a bear hug, giving her what Joe thought was an alarmingly rough shake in the process, yet Kate just laughed.

They were invited to be seated. Joe helped Kate into her chair and slid into his just as the happy couple arrived to rousing applause, holding each other's hands. As they dined on filet of beef, the couple was toasted with champagne for a lifetime of happiness.

Then it was Kiefer's turn to speak. "I'm not very good at this," he said, taking the mic and standing. "But as a lot of you know, I've been around awhile."

Someone in the back hooted at that, and Kiefer laughed. "Keep it down back there, Bryan. So anyway, I've been around awhile. I've had my fair share of relationships, but you know, I knew something was different when I met Lisa. I don't know if I could put a word to it, but I knew, deep down, that she was The One. To my beautiful bride," he said, and leaned down to kiss her.

In the midst of a lot of oohing and aahing and cries of "Hear, hear," Joe and Kate exchanged a look. He saw the blush come up in her cheeks and felt a strange little swirl of recognition in his gut.

"My turn!" Lisa said loudly, and several people chuckled. She took the mic from her husband. "As several of you know, I almost killed Kiefer this week."

The crowd laughed.

"But honestly, I can't imagine life without him. My hope is that everyone here gets to experience the love we have for each other." She suddenly turned and looked directly at Kate and Joe. "Right, Kate?" she asked, and the crowd laughed again.

"Oh my god, she didn't just do that, did she?" Kate muttered under her breath to Joe.

"She did," he muttered back.

When the speeches were done and the toasts concluded, the band began to play. Everyone gathered around the dance floor and watched Lisa dance with her father, then with Kiefer. They swayed back and forth, sharing a private laugh.

When everyone was invited to join the dance, Joe looked at Kate and held out his hand. "Do you dance?"

"Do I dance!" she said, as if she danced for the ballet, and slipped her hand into his. "Not really."

Joe laughed. "Then that makes two of us."

He led her out onto the dance floor, took her hand and tucked it in between them, pulled her in close, and began to move.

"Hey," Kate said as they moved languidly around the dance floor. "You're a good dancer. I would not have guessed that about you."

There was so much about him that she didn't know, that he wished she knew. "What? Didn't you see me leap over the rope at the Hertz counter?"

"That was more like a hurdle," she reminded him.

"You're not so bad yourself," he said. There was an easy grace to her. "By the way," he said, "I finished your book."

She gasped with surprise; her eyes glittered happily. "When?"

"This afternoon. I had a little downtime."

"So what did you think?"

"Want to know the truth?" he asked.

Her smile faded a little. "Yes," she said. "I do." She looked as if she expected him to say something disparaging.

"I didn't want it to end," Joe said. "Don't look *that* surprised," he said, laughing at her shocked expression. "I liked those two. I wanted to know what happened after they resolved everything. What their children looked like, if she ever sorted things out with her mother."

"You *did*?"

Kate looked so happy, and Joe liked that he had made her look that way. "I did. I don't think I am going to break my lifelong habit of sticking to magazines and tech manuals, but yes, I really enjoyed it and didn't want it to end. Do you ever feel that way?" he asked, referring to the books she edited.

Something flickered in Kate's gaze. "Yes," she said. "Actually, I'm sort of feeling that way now."

Joe sighed and pulled her in a little closer. "Me too, baby."

"You know, some might argue that this thing between us doesn't have to end, but..." Her voice trailed off. She looked a little hopeful, and that made Joe uneasy.

"But I'm here, at a new job," he said. "And you're in New York."

"And long distance never really works, does it?" she said sadly.

"Even if it did, east coast–west coast is not an easy distance to work with."

The music was ending. Kate glanced down and nodded. "I just wish... I just wish you weren't such a great guy, Joe Firretti. I wish you'd turned out to be the armrest hog from hell, you know?"

Joe couldn't help but laugh. "I kind of wish I had, too," he said. He didn't like feeling as helpless and hopeless as he was right now. But he was determined not to let the evening end on a somber note. "Let's make the best of tonight."

Kate's smile returned. "What'd you have in mind?"

"Champagne to start. Then you, naked. Me, admiring you, naked." He grinned, his body stirring at just the suggestion.

"I think that could be arranged," she said coyly.

"But we have to be careful. My parents have the ears of donkeys. And you might have to jackhammer me out of this dress."

"That," he said, leaning forward, putting his mouth to her temple, "will be my great pleasure."

———

At half past two in the morning, Joe was lying on a cot in the library at the Preston house, his arms folded behind his head. He'd given up on Kate and figured she'd gotten cold feet in her parents' house.

But then he heard the door. He sat up, saw her slip into the library wearing a flannel pajama top that came to the top of her thighs. She closed the door very carefully behind her, then tiptoed quickly across the floor and hopped on top of him. She instantly covered his mouth with her hand. *"Shhh,"* she whispered.

Joe nodded, slipped his hand under her top, and closed his eyes as his fingers slid over smooth, warm skin. Kate began to kiss him, sinking down onto his body, her hands sliding through his hair, down his side.

Joe had the hazy thought that this was what it was supposed to be like, that the times before Kate had been nothing, just diversions, a passing of time. And when he entered her, and slid into that state of pure, pleasurable oblivion, he could think only that this was right, this was *so* right.

So right that it was screwed up.

Chapter 11

KATE WOKE TO THE SOUND OF SOMEONE rummaging around in the kitchen. She felt Joe warm on her back, his body spooned around hers. She could hear the patter of rain on the roof and wanted nothing more than to burrow deep under the covers and pretend there wasn't a world out there, or two lives on different paths.

She twisted in Joe's arms to face him, kissed his chest. Last night had been magical. Surreal, even. She hated when authors described sex as surreal, because she could never imagine how it could be so. To her, sex had always been very concrete. But last night, she'd existed outside herself, had ridden along on an enormous wave of pleasure Joe gave her. He was an excellent lover, a man of many talents, and thinking about them made her smile. She kissed his lips gently and eased off the cot.

"Hey," he said groggily, reaching for her.

"Shh," she reminded him, and touched her fingers to his lips before scurrying across the library. She opened the door, listened for the sound of anyone coming her way, and stepped out.

By the time Joe appeared—showered and dressed—Kate's extended family was present and accounted for, grazing on the leftovers from the bridal banquet.

"Honey, leave your dress," Mom was saying as Joe sauntered in, clean-shaven and impossibly handsome. "Good morning, Joe! Did you sleep well?"

He glanced at Kate. "I slept *great*," he said, and Kate almost laughed.

"There's coffee," Kate's mother said, pointing to the pot. "Anyway," she continued in Kate's direction, "I'm going to have it cleaned and boxed."

"Why, Mom?" Kate asked. "I'm never wearing it again."

"Never say 'never.' There may come some event where you need a fancy evening gown."

"You could get married in it," Cassidy offered, wiggling her eyebrows at Kate.

"Mom," Kate said wearily.

"Cassidy, leave your sister alone. She is very sensitive about peach dresses."

Kate rolled her eyes at her little sister.

"Hey, did you hear the news this morning?"

Colton asked. "They say the strike will be settled today, the blizzard is about done, and air traffic should be almost normal by Tuesday. Airports are finally opening back up."

"I guess that means no trains or cars to New York this time, Katie-Kate," her father said with a chuckle. "So, Joe, when do you start work?"

"Ah... tomorrow," he said.

"Joe, have some beef filet," Kate's mother said, steering him in the direction of the buffet where the food had been laid out. "Never accuse the Prestons of being predictable in their breakfast choices."

"Thank you," Joe said uncertainly, and peered into the big aluminum pan.

"He doesn't have to eat that," Kate tried, but her mother was already waving her away.

"He doesn't mind, do you, Joe? Live on the edge, I say."

"So life goes back to normal for you two, I guess," Kate's father said from behind the morning paper.

"Oh, but Joe will come for dinner now and then, won't you, Joe?" Kate's mother chimed in.

Joe smiled, but Kate could see he wasn't feeling it. She wasn't either. What would be the point? "I'll sure try," he said, and thank God, that seemed to satisfy Kate's mom.

"It's such a shitty day," Cassidy complained.

"Language!" Kate's mother said sternly.

"Hey, Joe, do you play cards?" Colton asked. "We like to play Spades on days like this."

Kate expected him to say no, that he had to go, but Joe surprised her. With a plate laden with filet of beef and twice-baked potato, he said, "Sure!"

They spent the day with Kate's family playing cards, then working on an enormous puzzle her father had started in the dining room, and occasionally glanced at the big picture window and the rain rivulets racing down the glass.

The air felt heavy. Kate had felt a weight pressing on her all day. She knew what it was—it was the sense of an impending loss.

Late in the afternoon, as her family buzzed around the kitchen and the living area, Joe looked at Kate with sorrow in his eyes, and she knew the moment of loss had come. "I should go," he said.

Her heart sank. This was it, then, the end to the most wildly adventurous, sexy, fabulous few days she'd ever spent. "I don't want to say good-bye," she muttered helplessly.

"Then don't say it," he said, and intertwined his fingers with hers. "It's not good-bye, Kate. We'll talk, right?"

She nodded.

"What's going on?" Cassidy asked, her insanely accurate radar honing in on Joe and Kate. "Are you taking off, Joe?"

"Yeah," he said, coming to his feet. "I have an early day tomorrow." He walked away from Kate to say his good-byes to her family.

There was a lot of promising to get together, to include Joe in family gatherings in the weeks to come. But Kate didn't believe it. Her family meant well, as did Joe. But people were busy, and she could picture her family gathered here on a Sunday afternoon, and someone would mention Joe, and someone else would say, "Oh yeah, I meant to give him a call," and that would be followed by, "Let's Skype with Kate later."

And as the days and weeks went on, they would forget about him entirely. But Kate would never forget him. Never.

The rain had let up when she walked him outside. A cab was waiting at the bottom of the drive. Kate stood with her hands on her back, Joe with his hands shoved into the pockets of his jeans.

She looked at the cab, then at him. "Do you believe in fate, yet?"

He smiled wryly.

"Me either," she said. "Because if this is fate, fate sucks."

"I couldn't agree more." He shifted forward, putting his arms around her.

"Will you call me when you're in New York?" she asked in almost a whisper.

"Yes. And you'll call me when you're in Seattle, right?"

"Yes."

Joe leaned back and cupped her face. He peered into her eyes, and it felt to Kate as if he was trying to commit her to memory somehow. She reached up and wrapped her fingers around his wrist. "How can I miss you so much already when I hardly know you?"

He sighed, lowered his head, and kissed her. It was a tender, emotional kiss, and when he lifted his head, Kate dabbed at the lone tear that fell from the corner of one eye.

"I'll talk to you soon. Tomorrow, maybe." He dropped his arms from her. "Kate... I've never met anyone like you before. Thanks for... this," he said, gesturing to the two of them. "Seems so inadequate to say, but I mean it."

She knew exactly what he meant. She'd known him for all of four days now, and yet she felt like she was losing her very best friend. She shoved her hands into the back pockets of her pants to keep from grabbing on to him and holding him here. She willed herself not to get girly and teary. "Good-bye, Joe Firretti."

"Good-bye, Kate Preston."

She watched him walk down to the end of the drive. He opened the cab door and paused. He looked back at her before he got in.

Kate lifted her hand and waved.

She didn't know if he waved back because she couldn't see much through the tears that had filled her eyes.

Chapter 12

KATE HAD BEEN BACK IN NEW YORK FOR TWO weeks, and still the feeling of heaviness had not lifted from her. She'd thought that after she'd regaled the editorial staff with her wild tale of her trip to Seattle, she would fall into work and everything would fade into a warm, soft memory.

Maybe it would have, had Kate and Joe not spoken regularly.

She knew the head guy at his new company seemed impressed by Joe, and that he had a corner office. She knew he liked running in Discovery Park and he didn't like that it rained so much. He knew she had finished editing the novel he'd read and had just closed a deal for another one. They were talking, but Kate could feel a distance developing there, the inevitable flow of life carrying them away from each other. The further they drifted, the heavier the weight felt to her.

And yet, she couldn't seem to shake him. She walked to work and envisioned the dangerously handsome man who had appeared at Lisa's wedding in a dark suit, clean-shaven, and with that cute little pocket square. She walked home from work and looked at each man who passed her, trying to find one who would appeal to her the way Joe had. None of them did.

Kate still didn't know if she believed in fate, but if she did, she would want to know what exactly it was trying to do to her. Right now, she hated fate. She wanted to kick fate's ass.

One morning, seated in her cubbyhole between stacks of manuscripts and books, Kate was making herself especially crazy. Lisa was back from her two-week honeymoon and had bombarded Facebook with pictures of a tropical paradise. There was Kiefer looking toned and buff, Lisa tanned and slim.

They looked so damn happy, and that made Kate even sadder. Before she'd gotten on that plane, she wouldn't have said that marriage or commitment was at the top of her list. It hovered there somewhere, she supposed, but she'd been too focused on the move to New York, on her job, on settling in. Now, that idea was front and center. Now, she knew the void that existed in her life. It had taken the trip to show her just how much she did want love and marriage and more.

After work that day, Kate was coaxed into happy hour with a couple of people, and then to a sushi bar. She recognized the name of it—Joe had told her about it.

She returned home to her tiny walk-up apartment and looked around. Why did she think this would be so great? It looked small and dingy and... and empty. So damn empty.

The next morning, Kate more or less dragged herself to work and spent a day in meetings. By the time she was ready to go home, it had started to rain. Perfect, she thought morosely. Rain was perfect for her black mood.

She found her battered umbrella at the bottom of her bag, said good night to the security guard, and walked outside. She stood under the awning for a long moment, debating. Which would be crazier? A very crowded subway? Or trying to hail a cab?

She decided the subway was her only hope and started down the street, almost colliding with a man just standing there. Why was he standing there in the rain? Kate shot him a look—and then came to an abrupt halt.

Joe.

She was so surprised that her umbrella dropped. He caught it with his hand and propped it back up over her head. She couldn't speak; her heart was in her throat. He looked as amazing as he did in her mind's eye, every inch of him, every bit of blue in his eyes.

"Hey," he said, looking her up and down. "Don't I know you from somewhere?"

Kate stepped closer, her heart beating wildly. "Weren't you the guy sitting next to me on the plane, totally hogging the armrest?"

"Right, right," he said, smiling down at her, his eyes dancing with delight. "I remember you now. You were clogging the aisles with a big pink raft."

"What are you doing here?" she asked.

"I came to ask if you believe in fate."

Kate's breath caught.

"Because I do," he said.

"You do?"

"Yeah, I do. I believe fate put me on that plane, and I think fate led me to the best few days of my life. I think fate knocked me over the head and showed me that maybe the greatest opportunity of my life was standing right in front of me in a hideous bridesmaid dress. And I couldn't ignore her, because fate is one persistent bitch."

"Yes, yes, I know," Kate said, nodding furiously. "She's really awful." Her heart was filling up with wild, crazy hope, filling up so fast that she could hardly breathe. "So you leaped across the country to tell me that?"

Joe shook his head. He slipped his arm around her waist and drew her in to him. "I leaped to be with you, Kate."

Her heart was beating so wildly she feared she would sink to her knees. This was crazy, insane! "Wait… what about your job?"

"You know, it was an amazing opportunity," he said. "But it's not so amazing without someone to share it with. So I called my old boss and asked him for my job back."

Kate gasped.

"That call turned out pretty well. He was so thrilled to have me back that he gave me more money. Turns out, my position is pretty hard to fill."

"But what about your new job?"

Joe winced. "They weren't quite as thrilled. I think it's safe to say they were pissed. Words like 'lawsuit' and 'breach' were tossed around."

"Joe!"

"Not to worry," he said. "I hadn't signed the contract yet."

"You're moving back to New York?" she asked, afraid to believe it.

"Baby, I'm already back," he said with a wink. "And I could use a place to stay for a couple of nights."

It was a dream come true, a private hope brought to life. Kate dropped her umbrella and threw her arms around his neck and kissed him. She kissed him hard, with all the weight she'd been feeling these last few weeks. She was oblivious to the rain, oblivious to the people sailing past them. If this were a movie, little stars would burst over her head and blue birds would flit about them.

Joe was laughing when she lifted her head. "I guess that's a yes," he said.

"I love you, Joe. I know I'm not supposed to say that because I just met you, but I do, Joe, I *do*. I *love* you."

"God, Kate, I love you, too," he said, burying his face in her neck. "I should have told you two weeks ago. I should never have gotten in that cab. Come on, let's get out of the rain."

He stooped down to pick up her umbrella. He put his arm around her waist and pulled her into his side. "What about ESP? Do you believe in that?" he asked.

Kate laughed. "It depends."

She believed in love. That much, she knew, and here it was, delivered by fate to her, all six feet, two inches of it.

Chapter 13

ONE YEAR LATER, ON A WET SPRING WEEKEND, Joe and Kate were married in Seattle. Lisa stood up with Kate, wearing a lovely off-the-shoulder lavender gown, which Lisa proclaimed too plain and too predictable. The reception was held at a new venue: an industrial building that had been transformed inside to look like an art museum. Or maybe it was an art museum. Joe had lost track of the details.

He was happy. Happier than he thought he could be. He was frankly amazed at how damn happy he was.

Kate was happy, too. She was still amused and awed that things had happened as they had, that she'd met the man of her dreams on a flight diverted to Dallas. She was awed that she and Joe had both known, in just a few days, just *knew*, that they belonged together. What would explain that other than fate? Kate hoped that fate also had a big family in mind for them, now that she knew Joe wasn't particularly put off by people wandering in and out of the house without knocking and raiding the fridge, as her family tended to do.

They stayed at the Edgewater the night of the wedding, and their lovemaking was spectacular. The next morning they made their way to Kate's house, where the Firrettis and the Prestons had come together to dine on leftover wedding food for breakfast before the newlyweds headed off to Paris for their honeymoon. While they were dining, the clouds rolled in, swallowing up the sun.

Later still, when Colton drove them to the airport, the clouds were hanging even heavier. Kate and Joe joked about late spring blizzards and air traffic controller strikes.

The newly minted Mr. and Mrs. Firretti checked their bags. "Are you sure you want to carry that on?" Joe asked, looking at the enormous tote bag Kate was holding. "Yes," she said. "It's got everything we need. Books, iPad, toothbrushes, change of underwear—"

"Okay, okay," he said. "Just please don't tell me it has a tuna-fish sandwich in it."

"No!" Kate said. "I'll buy that at a kiosk or something." She smiled at his look of horror.

They made it through security and wandered up to their gate. They glanced up at the board. *Delayed*, it said.

"Wait here," Joe said, and walked up to the counter and spoke to the airline agent. He returned a moment later, a funny little smile on his face.

"So what's the delay?" Kate asked.

"Indefinite. Seems there is an unexpected weather event in Europe and the plane coming in is being diverted."

Kate blinked. And Mr. and Mrs. Firretti burst into laughter.

Thinking of You

by Jill Mansell

———

When Ginny Holland's daughter heads off to university, Ginny is left with a severe case of empty nest syndrome. To make matters worse, the first gorgeous man she's laid eyes on in years has just accused Ginny of shoplifting. So, in need of a bit of company, Ginny decides to advertise for a lodger, but what she gets is lovelorn Laurel. Yet with Laurel comes her dangerously charming brother, Perry, and the offer of a great new job, and things begin looking up…until Ginny realizes that her potential boss is all too familiar. Is it too late for Ginny to set things right after an anything but desirable first impression?

———

Praise for **An Offer You Can't Refuse***:*

"Realistic, flawed, and endearing, [the characters] make Ms. Mansell's book shine." —*Romance Reader at Heart*

"A finely tuned romantic comedy." —*Kirkus*

For more Jill Mansell, visit:

www.sourcebooks.com

Don't Want to Miss a Thing

Jill Mansell

—⁓—

He knows all about women, or so he thought…

Dexter Yates leads a charmed existence in London, with money, looks, and girlfriends galore. Life's fantastic until Dex's sister dies and his world changes overnight. Astonishing everyone, including himself, Dex leaves the city behind, takes charge of his eight-month-old niece Delphi, moves to a beautiful Cotswolds village, and sets about working on his parenting skills. His neighbors, including cartoonist Molly Hayes, seem friendly enough—but Dex can't shake the notion that he's missing something important…

—⁓—

Praise for Thinking of You:

"Mansell is like a Michelin-rated chef: She may use common ingredients, but under her sure hand, the results are deliciously superior." —*Kirkus*

"Humorous, sometimes poignant… Her breezy style resembles that of Sophie Kinsella or Helen Fielding… readers will be delighted." —*Booklist*

"Jill Mansell has never let me down and she delivers once again… had me laughing and smiling from beginning to end." —*Life in the Thumb*

For more Jill Mansell, visit:

www.sourcebooks.com

A Royal Pain

by Megan Mulry

—◦◦◦—

A life of royalty seems so attractive…until you're invited to live it…

Smart, ambitious, and career driven, Bronte Talbot started following British royalty in the gossip mags only to annoy her intellectual father. But her fascination has turned into a not-so-secret guilty pleasure. When she starts dating a charming British doctoral student, she teases him unmercifully about the latest scandals of his royal countrymen, only to find out—to her horror—that she's been having a fling with the nineteenth Duke of Northrop, and now he wants to make her…a duchess?

In spite of her frivolous passion for all things royal, Bronte isn't at all sure she wants the reality. Is becoming royalty every American woman's secret dream, or is it a nightmare of disapproving dowagers, paparazzi, stiff-upper-lip tea parties, and over-the-top hats?

—◦◦◦—

"Laugh-out-loud funny with super sexy overtones." —*Catherine Bybee*, New York Times *bestselling author of* Wife by Wednesday

"Take one sparky, sailor-mouthed American girl and one handsome English aristocrat. Put them together and watch the sparks fly. Sizzling fun!" —*Jill Mansell*, New York Times *bestselling author of* Nadia Knows Best

For more Megan Mulry, visit:

www.sourcebooks.com

If the Shoe Fits

Megan Mulry

—◆◆◆—

The only thing worse than being in the spotlight is being kept in the dark…

With paparazzi nipping at his heels, Devon Heyworth, rakish brother of the Duke of Northrop, spends his whole life hiding his intelligence and flaunting his playboy persona. Fast cars and faster women give the tabloids plenty to talk about.

American entrepreneur Sarah James is singularly unimpressed with "The Earl" when she meets him at a wedding. But she's made quite an impression on him. When he pursues her all the way across the pond, he discovers that Miss James has no intention of being won over by glitz and glamour—she's got real issues to deal with, and the last thing she needs is larger-than-life royalty mucking about in her business…

—◆◆◆—

Praise for **A Royal Pain***:*

"A romantic, fantastic, enchanting treat… Don't miss *A Royal Pain*!" —Eloisa James, *New York Times* bestselling author of *The Ugly Duchess*

"Megan Mulry is a must-read author. Highly recommended." —Jennifer Probst, *New York Times* bestselling author of *The Marriage Mistake*

For more Megan Mulry, visit:

www.sourcebooks.com

Sultry with a Twist

by Macy Beckett

—〰—

Welcome to Sultry Springs, Texas:
where first loves find second chances…

Nine years after June Augustine hightailed it out of Sultry Springs with her heart in pieces, one thing stands between her and her dream of opening an upscale martini bar: a bogus warrant from her tiny Texas hometown. Now she's stuck in the sticks for a month of community service under the supervision of the devilishly sexy Luke Gallagher, her first love and ex-best friend.

If Texas wasn't already hot enough, working side-by-side with June would make any man melt. Luke wants nothing more than to strip her down and throw her in the lake—the same lake where they were found buck naked and guilty as sin all those years ago. In their heads, they're older and wiser. But their hearts tell a different story…

—〰—

"Witty and fun, warm and endearing,
Macy Beckett will tug your heartstrings!"
—*Carly Phillips*, New York Times *bestselling author*

"Fun and flirty with characters you'll love page after page."
—*Christie Craig*, New York Times *bestselling author*

For more Macy Beckett, visit:

www.sourcebooks.com

A Shot of Sultry

by Macy Beckett

—∿∿—

Welcome to Sultry Springs, Texas: where home can be the perfect place for a fresh start.

For West Coast filmmaker Bobbi Gallagher, going back to Sultry Springs is a last resort. But with her career in tatters, a documentary set in her hometown might be just what she needs to salvage her reputation. She just can't let anything distract her again. Not even the gorgeous contractor her brother asked to watch over her. As if she can't handle filming a few rowdy Texans.

Golden boy Trey Lewis, with his blond hair and Technicolor-blue eyes, is a leading man if Bobbi ever saw one. He's strong and confident and—much to her delight—usually shirtless. He thinks keeping his best friend's baby sister out of trouble will be easy. But he has no idea of the trouble in store for *him*…

—∿∿—

"A heartwarming, humorous story of second chances…sweet at its core. A strong continuation of this promising series." —*Publishers Weekly*

"Brimming with rapier wit and heartwarming moments… Packed with humor and heart." —*Fresh Fiction*

For more Macy Beckett, visit:

www.sourcebooks.com

New York Times and *USA Today* bestselling author

Rev It Up
Black Knights Inc.

by Julie Ann Walker

———

He's the heartbreaker she left behind…

Jake "the Snake" Sommers earned his SEAL code name by striking quickly and quietly—and with lethal force. That's also how he broke Michelle Carter's heart. It was the only way to keep her safe—from himself. Four long years later, Jake is determined to get a second chance. But to steal back into Michelle's loving arms, Jake is going to have to prove he can take things slow. Real slow…

Michelle Carter has never forgiven Jake for being so cliché as to "love her and leave her." But when her brother, head of the Black Knights elite ops agency, pisses off the wrong mobster, she must do the unimaginable: place her life in Jake's hands. No matter what they call him, this man is far from cold-blooded. And once he's wrapped around her heart, he'll never let her go…

———

Praise for **Hell on Wheels***:*

For more Black Knights Inc., visit:

www.sourcebooks.com

New York Times and *USA Today* bestselling author

Thrill Ride

by Julie Ann Walker

———

He's gone rogue

Ex-Navy SEAL Rock Babineaux's job is to get information, and he's one of the best in the business. Until something goes horribly wrong and he's being hunted by his own government. Even his best friends at the covert special-ops organization Black Knights Inc. aren't sure they can trust him. He thinks he can outrun them all, but his former partner—a curvy bombshell who knows just how to drive him wild—refuses to cut him loose.

She won't back down

Vanessa Cordera hasn't been the team's communication specialist very long, but she knows how to read people—no way is Rock guilty of murder. And she'll go to hell and back to help him prove it. Sure, the sexy Cajun has his secrets, but there's no one in the world she'd rather have by her side in a tight spot. Which is good, because they're about to get very tight...

———

Praise for the Black Knights Inc. series:

"Walker is ready to join the ranks of great romantic suspense writers." —*RT Book Reviews*

For more Black Knights Inc., visit:

www.sourcebooks.com

A Wedding in Apple Grove

by C.H. Admirand

———

He's not so sure about small town life.
She can't imagine living anywhere else.

Welcome to Apple Grove, Ohio (population 597), where everyone has your best interests at heart, even if they can't agree on the best way to meddle. When the townsfolk of Apple Grove need handiwork done, there's no job too small for the Mulcahy sisters: Megan, Caitlin, and Grace.

Specializing in hard work and family loyalty, tomboy Meg Mulcahy has left behind any girlhood dreams of romance. Enter newcomer Daniel Eagan, looking to bury his own broken heart and make a new start. He's surprised—and delighted—by the winsome girl with the mighty tool belt who shows up to fix his wiring.

But Dan's got a lot to learn about life in a small town, and when Meg's past collides with her future, it may take all 595 other residents of Apple Grove to keep this romance from short-circuiting.

———

"Sexy and fun… Admirand's series will be popular, especially with fans of Susan Wiggs and Janet Chapman." —*Booklist*

For more C.H. Admirand, visit:

www.sourcebooks.com

One Day in Apple Grove

by C.H. Admirand

—◦◦◦—

***Welcome to Apple Grove, Ohio (population 597),
a small town with a big heart.***

Caitlin Mulcahy loves her family. She really does. But sometimes they can drive her to her last shred of sanity—from her dad ("I'm not meddling, I just want what's best for you") to her eight-months-pregnant older sister to her younger sister, who will do just about anything to avoid real work. Cait just needs to get away, even if for only an hour.

When she sees someone in need of help on the side of the road, of course she's going to pull over. She might even be able to fix his engine—after all, the Mulcahy family is a handy bunch. She's not expecting that former Navy medic Jack Gannon and a little black puppy named Jameson will be the ones who end up rescuing her…

—◦◦◦—

"For fans of Susan Wiggs and Janet Chapman." —*Booklist*

For more C.H. Admirand, visit:

www.sourcebooks.com

SEALed with a Ring

by Mary Margret Daughtridge

———

She's got it all… except the one thing she needs most

Smart, successful businesswoman JJ Caruthers has a year to land a husband or lose the empire she's worked so hard to build. With time running out, romance is not an option, and a military husband who is always on the road begins to look like the perfect solution…

He's a wounded hero with an agenda of his own

Even with the scars of battle, Navy SEAL medic Davy Graziano is gorgeous enough to land any woman he wants, and he's never wanted to be tied down. Now Davy has ulterior motives for accepting JJ's outrageous proposal of marriage, but he only has so long to figure out what JJ doesn't want him to know…

———

Praise for SEALed with a Ring:

"With a surprising amount of heart, Daughtridge makes a familiar story read like new as the icy JJ melts under Davy's charm during a forced marriage. The supporting cast, including one really unattractive dog, makes Daughtridge's latest one for the keeper shelves." —*RT Book Reviews*, 4 stars

For more Mary Margret Daughtridge, visit:

www.sourcebooks.com

SEALed Forever

by Mary Margret Daughtridge

—◦◦◦—

He's got a living, breathing dilemma…

In the midst of running an undercover CIA mission, Navy SEAL Lt. Garth Vale finds an abandoned baby, and his superiors sure don't want to know about it. The only person who can help him is the beautiful new doctor in town, but she's got another surprise for him…

She's got a solution… at a price…

Dr. Bronwyn Whitescarver has left the frantic pace of big city ER medicine for a small town medical practice. Her bags aren't even unpacked yet when gorgeous, intense Garth Vale shows up on her doorstep in the middle of the night with a sick baby…

But his story somehow doesn't add up, and Bronwyn isn't quite sure who she's saving—the baby, or the man…

—◦◦◦—

Praise for **SEALed Forever***:*

"Take two strong characters, throw in some humor and a baby, and you've got a perfect combination for a heartwarming romance. The suspense subplot is a bonus in this well-written story." —*RT Book Review*, 4.5 stars

For more Mary Margret Daughtridge, visit:

www.sourcebooks.com

The Officer Breaks the Rules

by Jeanette Murray

———∿∿———

He's ruled by loyalty…

Every man knows that you don't date your best friend's little sister, but Captain Jeremy Phillips can't seem to convince Madison O'Shay to stay away. And he can't convince himself to stop thinking about her, either.

She's ruled by love…

Madison knows exactly what she wants… and whom. But she won't give up her career in the Navy for any man, not even Jeremy.

They're both about to learn that in the game of love, it's all about breaking the rules.

———∿∿———

"If you are looking for sexy, edgy, gripping series that will keep you invested and turning pages, look no further. You will absolutely love this one." —*Guilty Pleasures Book Reviews*

"I just loved *The Officer Breaks the Rules*. I fell in love with the characters from the first book in the series and continued to fall in love with them in this book." —*Night Owl Reviews*

For more Jeanette Murray, visit:

www.sourcebooks.com

The Officer and the Secret

by Jeanette Murray

—◦◦◦—

If there's one thing he hates, it's a secret…

Coming home after a rough deployment, Captain Dwayne Robertson wants some stability in his life, and finds it in the friendship he's forged with Veronica Gibson while he was away. But her past is a well-guarded mystery, and Dwayne doesn't know if he can deal with a woman who has something to hide…

And she's filled with them…

Veronica Gibson doesn't want anyone to know about her bizarre upbringing. She's finally escaped her missionary parents and would be enjoying her independence if she didn't feel so insecure about fitting in. She can easily envision a glorious future with Dwayne—but can she build a new life on a web of lies?

—◦◦◦—

Praise for Jeanette Murray:

"Her characters and their challenges are relatable, and will inspire readers to fight for what they want in their own lives." —*RT Book Reviews*

For more Jeanette Murray, visit:

www.sourcebooks.com

A SEAL at Heart

by Anne Elizabeth

He lost just about everything on that mission…

Being a Navy SEAL means everything to John "Red Jack" Roaker, but a mission gone wrong has left his buddy dead, his memory spotty, and his world turned upside down. His career as a SEAL is threatened unless Dr. Laurie Smith's unconventional methods of therapy can help him.

Maybe she can show him how to get it back…

Laurie's father was a SEAL—and she knows exactly what the personal cost can be. She can't resist trying everything to help this man, and not only because she finds him as sexy as he is honorable.

As the layers of Jack's resistance peel away, he and Laurie unearth secrets that go to the highest levels of the military— and the deepest depths of their hearts…

"A romance with real heart, from a talented writer who has deep personal insight into what it takes to be a Navy SEAL." —*New York Times* bestselling author Suzanne Brockmann

"Two wounded souls find healing through love… Readers will find this book an accurate reflection of what's happening in the world today and perhaps be uplifted by its message of hope." —*Booklist*

For more Anne Elizabeth, visit:

www.sourcebooks.com

Once a SEAL

Anne Elizabeth

—◦◦◦—

A hero of her own

What woman hasn't dreamed of what it would be like to marry a Navy SEAL? Dan McCullum is everything Aria has ever imagined—sweet, strong, and sexy as hell. She just never expected how tough the SEAL life would be. Dan could be gone at a moment's notice and not allowed to tell her where he's going or when he'll be back.

Dan has never backed down from a challenge in his life. But this one is his hardest yet: How does he balance his duty to his country with a soul-deep love for Aria? It's going to require patience, ingenuity, and some of the hottest homecomings he can dream up. Because for him, this isn't a fling; this is forever…

—◦◦◦—

Praise for **A SEAL at Heart***:*

"A beautiful story." —*New York Times* bestselling author Suzanne Brockmann

"An exciting and poignant read." —*Night Owl Reviews* TOP PICK

"You will not find a better storyteller with such feeling for the hearts of our military warriors." —*Coffee Time Romance*

For more Anne Elizabeth, visit:

www.sourcebooks.com

Billion Dollar Cowboy

Carolyn Brown

—∿∿∿—

A billionaire can buy anything…

Colton Nelson was twenty-eight years old when he won the Texas Lottery and went from ranch hand to ranch owner overnight. Now he's desperate to keep the gold diggers away. It shouldn't be too hard to find a pretty girl and hire her to pretend to be his one-and-only.

Or can he?

Laura Baker's got mixed feelings about this—she's on the ranch to work, not to be arm candy. On the other hand, being stuck for a while in the boondocks with a gorgeous cowboy isn't half-bad.

What neither Colton nor Laura expects are the intensely hard lessons they have to learn about the real cost of love…

—∿∿∿—

For more Carolyn Brown, visit:

www.sourcebooks.com

The Cowboy's Christmas Baby

Carolyn Brown

—⁓—

**'*Tis the season for…*
A pistol-totin' woman who's no angel
A tough rancher who doesn't believe in miracles
Love that warms the coldest night

After a year in Kuwait, Lucas Allen can't wait to get back to his ranch for Christmas and meet his gorgeous Internet pal in person.

When he pulls in, there's Natalie Clark right in his front yard with a pink pistol in her hand and a dead coyote at her feet.

Lucas is unfazed. But wait…is that a BABY in her arms?

—⁓—

Praise for Carolyn Brown's Christmas cowboy romances:

"'Tis the season for hunky cowboys." —*RT Book Reviews*

"Carolyn Brown creates some handsome, hunkified, HOT cowboys! A fun, enjoyable four-star-Christmas-to-remember novel." —*The Romance Reviews*

"Makes me believe in Christmas miracles and long, slow kisses under the mistletoe." —*The Romance Studio*

For more Carolyn Brown, visit:

www.sourcebooks.com

The Summer He Came Home

Juliana Stone

—∿∿—

Sometimes the best place to find love is right back where you started…

Falling asleep in a different bed every night has made it easy for Cain Black to forget his past. It's been ten years since he packed his guitar and left Crystal Lake, Michigan, to chase his dreams. Now tragedy has forced him home again. And though Cain relishes the freedom of the road, one stolen moment with Maggie O'Rourke makes him wonder if he's missing out on something bigger than fame.

For Maggie—single mother and newly settled in Crystal Lake—love is a luxury she just can't afford. Sure, she appreciates the tall, dark, and handsome looks of prodigal son Cain Black. But how long can she expect the notorious hellion to stay?

The last thing either of them wants is something complicated. But sometimes love has its own plans.

—∿∿—

"Everything I love in a book: a hot and tender romance and a bad-boy hero to die for!" —Molly O'Keefe, author of *Can't Buy Me Love*

For more Juliana Stone, visit:

www.sourcebooks.com

The Christmas He Loved Her

by Juliana Stone

—◁◁◁—

His best gift this Christmas is her.

In the small town of Crystal Lake, Christmas is a time for sledding, hot chocolate, and cozying up to the fire. For Jake Edwards, it shouldn't be a time to give in to the feelings he's always had for Raine—especially since she's his brother's widow.

No one annoys Raine quite like her brother-in-law does. But when Jake brings home a tall blond thing from the city who's bad news, Raine needs to stop him from making the biggest mistake of his life. Does Raine want this woman to leave Crystal Lake because she's all wrong for Jake? Or is it because she wants him for herself…?

—◁◁◁—

Praise for **The Summer He Came Home***:*

"Everything I love in a book: a hot and tender romance and a bad-boy hero to die for!" —Molly O'Keefe, author of *Can't Buy Me Love*

For more Juliana Stone, visit:

www.sourcebooks.com

About the Author

Julia London is the *New York Times* and *USA Today* bestselling author of more than two dozen novels, including the Cedar Springs contemporary series, the Secrets of Hadley Green historical romance series, and numerous other works. She is a four-time finalist for the prestigious RITA Award for excellence in romantic fiction, and RT Book Club Award recipient for Best Historical Romance. She lives in Austin, Texas.